Essential items

Essential items

and Other Tales from a Land in Lockdown

Udayan Mukherjee

BLOOMSBURY

NEW DELHI • LONDON • OXFORD • NEW YORK • SYDNEY

BLOOMSBURY INDIA
Bloomsbury Publishing India Pvt. Ltd
Second Floor, LSC Building No. 4, DDA Complex, Pocket C – 6 & 7,
Vasant Kunj, New Delhi 110070

BLOOMSBURY, BLOOMSBURY INDIA and the Diana logo are trademarks of Bloomsbury Publishing Plc

First published in India 2020
This edition published 2020

ISBN: PB: 978-93-90252-21-3; eBook: 978-93-90252-23-7

2 4 6 8 10 9 7 5 3 1

Typeset in Manipal Technologies Limited
Printed and bound in India by Replika Press Pvt. Ltd.

FSC www.fsc.org MIX Paper from responsible sources FSC® C016779

The Horror not to be surveyed –
But skirted in the Dark –
With Consciousness suspended –
And Being under Lock –
I fear me this – is Loneliness –
The Maker of the soul
Its Caverns and its Corridors
Illuminate – or seal –

'The Loneliness One Dare Not Sound'
by Emily Dickinson

For Tinnie.

Contents

1

A Life or Death Situation

'Run, run, Kallu, run! A body just arrived.'

'Body?' Kallu looked up from his *chillum*. 'The stuff has gone to your head, Shibu. Sit quietly; there's no body coming now. The wood dealers must be drunk and creating a racket.'

'No, I saw the van with my own eyes. I swear!' Shibu insisted.

'Van?' Kallu stirred; took a long, last drag and tapped the clay pipe on the ground. Out tipped a piece of glowing charcoal and some ash from the burnt ganja, which he proceeded to address. 'Your cremation is done, my friend. The ashes deserve to be floated in the river. Great joy you have spread during your short life.' Grinning at himself, he tucked the pipe into his waistband and stood up.

'Come then, let's see which great soul has reached our shores.'

Shibu wasn't fibbing. There was indeed a vehicle parked on the road outside the ghat.

Next to it, a hapless man tried to fend off the swarm of vendors who tugged at him from all directions.

'Sir, sir, the best sandalwood, you will get the fragrance from a mile away, this way please.'

'Here, you will need ghee for the service... pure cow ghee, not that fake tinned stuff.'

'What kind of flowers, marigold garlands, tuberose, how many sticks?'

Someone else stuck a bunch of incense sticks into the man's face, almost blinding him.

Kallu walked up and roared, 'Step back, you fucking vultures! Is this any way to accost a man who has lost a member of his family?'

The vendors stepped away. Kallu was kingpin of the *doms* at the ghat, a big fellow to boot; there was no messing with him.

'Namaste, *saab*. Please accept my condolences. You wish to cremate your...'

'Father,' the man said, looking warily into Kallu's bloodshot eyes.

'Oho, a father's demise, the most unbearable tragedy. That too, at a time like this. How difficult it must have been to arrange for the body to be brought here, no?'

This seemed to strike a chord with the man. Kallu made a quick assessment, as he always did with any prospective customer. Brahmin, middle-aged, reasonably prosperous. If Kallu had to guess, he would say mid-level official in some government office, with money in the family – a good prospect, for his purposes.

'Don't ask. I had to beg and plead, even pay an astronomical sum to the van owner as deposit, in case it got seized by the police on the way.'

'This is the problem with us, sir. One's misfortune is another's opportunity. No sense of solidarity. Don't know when we will ever learn. Why, look at all these guys converging on you to sell their wares.'

The vendors glowered at Kallu and there were faint murmurs of protest.

'Let me help you with this. Shibu!' he bellowed.

Shibu came running, palms folded.

'This is Shibu, a most capable *dom*. He will oversee the service. Shibu, call Saraswati and ask her to organize the holy fire.'

Then, turning to the vendors, Kallu picked them out, pointing with his finger, 'Modna, you get the sandalwood. Sir, sandalwood, right? A bit expensive, but for one's father… Lakhi, you do the flowers. Shibu, just buy the ghee and incense for sir, else they will pounce on him again.'

The man looked relieved.

'Thank you, bhai. Anything I can…'

'Oh, no no. That's between you and Shibu. We are like brothers. Your work is done, that is my satisfaction. Once it is all over, you, Shibu and I can take a short ride on my boat, immerse the ashes in the holy Ganges. Alright? Shibu, ensure everything is done properly.'

Kallu turned, winked at Shibu and marched off.

It was the first cremation in nearly three days at the Harishchandra ghat and there was none of the usual pandemonium. Everything happened as Kallu had ordained, and as the departed Mishraji's – that was his name – pyre was lit, sending flames leaping up into the gathering dusk sky, suffusing the ghats with an aroma of ghee, sandalwood and incense that subdued – sufficiently at least – the stench of charring flesh, the vendors stood around the fire looking suitably forlorn, chanting *Ram naam satya hai*, like a crowd of makeshift mourners. The dead man's son had come alone for the funeral and seemed glad for the company.

Once the fire had subsided, Shibu and Saraswati poked around the cinders and gathered the ashes into an earthen pot. Shibu cleared his throat and at his signal, Kallu lifted the urn and, with the most solemn of expressions on his face, brought it to young Mishraji.

'The mortal remains of your heavenly father, sir. Now, we must ensure they reach the gates of heaven. Please come with me.'

Kallu lowered the boat into the water, and the three of them took their places; Shibu and Kallu on either end with Mishraji in the middle, holding on to the urn. The sky had turned orange and they were the only ones on the river. They rowed on for a bit and at Kallu's signal, the man scattered his father's ashes into the river. As if on cue, the orange on the horizon faded to grey, lending an even greater poignancy to the setting. Mishraji wiped his eyes with his sleeve. Kallu let the boat drift in the river for a moment.

'Only a very lucky man gets a send-off like this, sir. All of us die, but not everyone is shown the way to the heavenly abodes. You have done your duty as a son, Mishraji. Your father's soul rests in peace.'

Mishraji regarded Kallu with tears in his eyes. Had it not been for the matter of awkward balance on the boat, he may even have forgotten his caste and hugged him. Behind his back, Shibu made a circle with his forefinger and thumb – good work.

Mishraji said, 'My sincere thanks to both of you. Honestly, I had expected it to be far more chaotic than this; that's what everyone had told me. But, it's so empty…'

Kallu smiled, sadly. 'You had heard right, sir. It can be a harrowing experience, but things are different now. In all my years at this ghat, and I have been here since I was a child, I have never seen a time like this. One cremation in three days! Usually, it's at least a dozen every day.'

'It's almost as if people have stopped dying in this country…' Shibu piped in.

Kallu gave him a stern look, as Mishraji tried to turn and look at Shibu, not managing it too well.

'Yes, I can imagine. Who would want the hassle of transporting a body at a time of lockdown? I was warned that the cops may stop the van and ask me to prove it wasn't a Muslim corpse; thankfully it didn't come to that. Sneaked through, somehow. But for all of you, this must be your source of income, right? How are you managing?' Mishraji asked.

Before Kallu could respond, Shibu – still on his own trip – blabbered, 'No, sir, it's not just the transport. Fewer people are dying too. So many of the bodies we get here are road and rail accident victims, all that has become zero. Even murders…'

Kallu tried to salvage the situation. 'You are right, of course, *saab*. Business is bad, but death brings such grief all around that I was telling Shibu just this morning, how does it matter if we earn less for a few days? At least there is less sorrow in the world. Isn't that something to be wished for?'

Mishraji seemed struck by Kallu's words.

'Such a nice thing to say. I'll never forget it. Maybe it's being on this river all day, with the spectre of death all around you...'

They had reached the banks.

Mishraji got out unsteadily, almost toppling over. Once he had recovered, he took out his wallet and asked Shibu, 'We didn't talk about the costs, how much should I...'

Shibu was about to quote a fee but Kallu intervened. 'Sir, don't embarrass us. This is not a marketplace, where we negotiate the price of things. There is only one father, one funeral for him... Whatever you think that is worth is fine with us.' Mishraji seemed speechless.

He mumbled, 'You know what, I'll just keep enough for the drive back and you take all of this.'

He had a thick wad of notes in his wallet, out of which he removed only a slim note to put in his breast pocket, handing the rest over to Kallu.

Kallu received it with folded hands and said, 'God be with you, sir. In our line, we never say, "hope to meet again"; but such is the cycle of life and death that maybe we will again someday. Tonight, Shibu and I will pray for your father's soul.'

Mishraji wiped his eyes again and walked away.

Once the van had left, Shibu said, 'Kallu, didn't you overdo it?'

'Shut up, you dimwit,' he said, flashing the notes. 'Look at this. Three days' loss made up in full.'

He counted the money.

'How much?'

'Twelve thousand. He paid the others separately?'

'Yes, Modna and Lakhi have been paid. I have to pay for the ghee, and Saraswati of course.'

'Okay, here is six for you.'

'But, Kallu, I did all the work...'

'See, this is the problem. You think he would have paid us a fraction of this had you jabbered on about road kills and murders? Huh? So many years you have been watching me, when will you learn something?'

Shibu grinned. It was true, he ought to be happy with the takings.

'Now go get a bottle. Tonight, we must sit on the riverbank and drink in prayer, to the smooth passage of Mishraji's ashes down the filth of this drain,' said Kallu with a flourish of his hand, inviting loud cackles from Shibu.

It was nearly half past eight in the evening when Shibu finally arrived, panting, bottle in hand. Kallu had been waiting for over an hour.

'*Chutiya*, where did you get your miserable ass stuck now? Brewing the hooch with your own hands, were you?'

'*Arrey*, who thought it would be so difficult to get liquor? All the shops are shut, they won't even slip one out the back door. Finally, I had to get one on loan from Budhia's house. Uff!'

'Loan?' Kallu sniggered. 'Very well, let's finish the bottle, refill it with sacred water and give it back; with one proper kick in the butt, as interest, from me. Loan, motherfucker!'

Shibu poured the liquid into two copper glasses, without spilling a drop. His eyes were used to the dark.

'No Coca Cola?'

'Here.' The big plastic bottle made a hiss as he turned the cap.

'*Jai bholenath*,' they raised their glasses.

The river bank was deserted, except for the two of them. Faint wisps of smoke rose from

Mishraji's pyre, though the fire was long dead. Next to it, they could make out the silhouette of a cow munching on marigold flowers.

'What a time. Never thought we would see days like this, really,' sighed Shibu.

'This may just be the trailer. Heaven knows how much longer we will have to suffer this. I meant to tell you earlier, Shibu, be very careful with money. What you got today, make it stretch a month. I am very worried.'

Shibu sat up. 'Really?'

'Why, weren't you yourself listing out the reasons for fewer customers to Mishraji's son? No roadkills, no crime... What is likely to change from tomorrow?'

'They will have to lift the lockdown. Else, more people will starve to death, Kallu. But dead bodies will mount, one way or the other.'

'Idiot. Since when did the poor get their dead to Kashi, to burn on sandalwood pyres? Have you lost your mind? Besides, these lockdowns will come and go; they will only make people think a hundred times before venturing out anywhere, least of all to places of cremation. What's to say that dead bodies with the virus aren't scattered on our banks?'

The thought alarmed Shibu, disturbing the slight buzz which had begun seeping into his head.

'Then?'

'Then what? We have to somehow tide over this phase; it's not as if we can suddenly start doing something else from tomorrow. We are fucking *doms*; between the two of us, we can't even read a death certificate!'

This banter was interrupted by a rustling sound of footsteps.

Instinctively, Shibu hid the liquor bottle between the folded legs of his lap.

'Kallu, I was looking for you.'

'Who is it?' Kallu strained to see. 'Oh, Shankar. We are having some rum, will you join us?' he asked, knowing full well that Shankar would never partake in drinking with a *dom*.

'No, no. There is a problem.'

'Of course, there is. Why else would you come looking for me at this hour? Someone died at the ashram, is it?'

Shankar was the long-standing caretaker-manager of the reputed Annapurna Mumukshu ashram – really an old age home – by the ghats. People came to die there, so that their ashes could be immersed in the river, with all their earthly sins forgiven by Lord Shiva. A death in Kashi was the most hallowed of exits any god-abiding Hindu could dream of. During Kallu's father's time as the head *dom*, the guests would die shortly after their arrival, but these days, they lived on for years before their wish was fulfilled. Business was good for Shankar; there was usually a long waiting list for rooms at the ashram. God's waiting room, Kallu had christened it.

'Yes, but it's not just that,' said Shankar, with a slight tremor in his voice.

Kallu shifted in his seat. Complicated situations interested him; they usually held potential for profit.

'Shankar, there is enough darkness all around, pray enlighten us, won't you?'

'You see, I had gone home over the last few days, because of this epidemic; Kanai was in charge at the ashram.'

'Kanai? Oh, that slow mutt? Something is wrong with him, you know, Shankar. The other day I saw him smearing his own forehead with cow dung.'

'Haha. Maybe he has realized that is what his fate holds,' Shibu quipped, sipping furtively as the men talked.

'So, I returned to find Kanai in a flap. Apparently, a couple from the ashram passed away today.'

'Together? How auspicious.'

'Hardly. Apparently, they had been running a fever for the last few days, coughing through the night.'

It took a moment for this to sink in. Kallu shouted, '*Behenchod*, now you say this? Step away right now, before I split your head with that oar!'

'What...what happened?' Shibu asked, confounded by this sudden eruption.

'You didn't hear? The two oldies who croaked had been ailing – fever, coughs. What does it sound like to you, duffer?'

'You mean, they had it?'

'What else? Why do you think Shankar is speaking to us as if he is a jilted lover? Bastard has two diseased corpses lying in his ashram. And he is probably infected too, by now. Step away, *saala*!'

Shankar retreated a few more steps. 'No, nothing has happened to me, Kallu. Look at me. I am fine. I didn't even enter their room, I swear. The moment Kanai told me, I had the same apprehensions, so I asked him to go back and lock the room, not tell anyone.'

Kallu glared at him. 'And how do you know Kanai didn't pass it on to you? The dunce must have been innocently tending to them the last few days. He has surely caught it.'

'I...I kept a distance when we spoke. There was no contact between us,' stammered Shankar.

'No contact! Listen to our scientist here! You don't need to fuck someone's ass to get the infection, you *chuth*. Just talking is enough.'

Shankar had no answer to this. Shibu, suitably alarmed by now, swung into the act. 'Shankar, leave us right now. Or else we won't be responsible for what happens next. Out!'

Shankar staggered backward and ran. Kallu had a reputation for being violent without provocation. Besides, his words had heightened Shankar's fears about his own health.

Once he vanished from sight, Kallu extended his glass. 'Forget the Coca Cola, just pour some rum. Maybe it will kill the germs. I have seen people pour it over their cuts in movies.'

Shibu wasn't sure if Kallu was pulling his leg, but he didn't think so.

'What did he want from us, you think?' he asked.

'Huh. What do people want from us, ass; to help read the palms of the dead? Shankar needs to dispose those bodies quickly, without anyone getting a whiff of it. Else, his ashram is history.'

Shibu nodded. After some consideration, he said, 'Shouldn't we at least check out how desperate he is? What if the families of the deceased are rich folk?'

Kallu turned to look at Shibu with something like respect in his eyes. 'First time in your life, you have spoken some sense. I may have finally rubbed off on you. But it's a risky venture.'

'No harm asking, is there?'

'True. Let's sleep over it tonight. With all this hooch, our heads are also not clear. At dawn tomorrow, let's discuss it again and if we agree, I will give Shankar a call. You have his phone number?'

Shibu nodded. He felt chuffed that Kallu was conferring with him, as if he were an equal.

He poured the rest of the rum out into the glasses. 'To the souls trapped in the locked room of the ashram...'

It was Kallu's turn to double up in laughter. He rolled back on to the damp ground and didn't budge again. Shibu followed. This was how they passed out on most nights – imbibe and lie back, allowing the gentle river breeze to lull them to sleep. Few possessions, fewer worries, Kallu liked to say.

When his eyes opened with the first rays of the sun, Kallu turned the scheme over in his head and came to a conclusion. He gave Shibu's inert body a kick.

Shibu groaned. 'Oho, you think Budhia may be stocking spurious stuff at home, Kallu? My head is splitting.'

'No, nothing wrong with the rum. I don't think we had dinner yesterday, that's the reason we are feeling like this. Have some hot jalebis and milk, you will be fine.'

At the mention of jalebis, Shibu sat up. An army of ants marched busily over the two glasses that lay upturned, feasting on the sticky remnants of the cola from last night. He shook them off and hauled himself up.

'Let me get them, then.'

By the time Shibu returned with a leaf packet of jalebis and glasses of milk, Kallu had worked out a plan.

'Didn't Saraswati have a bamboo stretcher… You know the ones in which we carry corpses sometimes?'

'Yeah, I think so. Like a ladder with a gunny sack in between the poles, right?'

'Yes, that one. Good, we'll need it.'

Kallu drained his glass and said, 'Call Shankar.'

Shibu called and handed Kallu the phone.

'Shankar? Still alive? I thought you may have joined the couple in your ashram. Listen, I have a plan. It's the only one which can work.'

'What?' Shankar asked.

'Call the relatives of the dead couple, tell them that both have died of the virus. There is no doubt about it. Where do they come from, by the way?'

'West Bengal, somewhere.'

'Excellent. So, there's no way they can get here immediately. Tell them no one here is prepared to touch the dead bodies, obviously. And you are contemplating just tossing them out on the street, because the other residents are panicking. With me, so far?'

'But no one knows...'

'Yes, donkey, but only you know that, not them. Improvise a bit. Scare them by saying that dogs will eat the bodies, or vultures will pick their eyes out. And then say, there just may be a way out.'

'What?'

'That you will use your connections to obtain a certificate saying the death was from natural causes, so that the last rites are not held up. More importantly, you have found, with great difficulty, two intrepid *doms*, who, with no care for their own well-being, have agreed to risk their lives and organize a proper cremation on the ghats, in the dead of night.'

'Oh, so you will do it... I knew it. Thank you, Kallu, thank you.'

'Quiet. Now we come to the crux of the plan. It will cost them. What do these good folks in Bengal do for a living?'

'Not sure... No, wait, the son is an advocate, I think. The one who came here two years ago.

He asked me how far the Allahabad High Court was from here, I remember.'

'Wonderful. So, they have money. Now listen carefully. You will tell them that the fee for this service will be 50,000 rupees per body, total one lakh.'

'What, one lakh?! But…' Shankar exclaimed.

'Yes, one lakh, not a rupee less. You tell me, what would a wealthy man choose, fifty thousand or the prospect of his mother's body being torn to pieces by wild dogs? And what is fifty thousand these days anyway – a phone costs that much. They will protest but agree. You are not to bring the price down.'

'Okay, I will try.'

'Good, and let us also be clear about the break up of this money. First, it is to be transferred to your account, today. Has to be today, else the bodies will rot, don't forget to mention that. So, as I was saying, 70 for Shibu and I, 10 to Bishu doctor for the death certificates – tell him to put heart attack, stroke, something serious – and 10 to Kanai. He is to be discharged from his duties and told to go back home, with this money. First thing tomorrow morning. Hope I don't need to explain why. And the remaining 10 is for you. Actually, you should get nothing; taking the bodies off your hands is a service big enough, but you can keep it as a goodwill gesture from our side.'

'But…'

'No buts, Shankar. If word gets out that there are two diseased corpses lying in your ashram, here is what happens – the rest of your guests run for their lives, the ashram is sealed indefinitely, your ass is hauled off to jail. And in future, your establishment will always be remembered as the corona ashram. In fact, it may become a mausoleum for tourists to see, from a distance. But you will never do business again. You still want to haggle with us over this?'

'No, no, Kallu. Let me just call them. I'll let you know.'

Kallu returned the phone to Shibu. 'Stick around, he will call back. I need to speak to him, give directions. His brain seems to have frozen up in fear. Happens.'

'One lakh, Kallu? Isn't that ambitious? I mean, will they be that desperate, you think?'

'My friend, it's not they who are desperate, but us. I don't know why you can't see it, but this disease is about to kick us in the stomach. Any day now, open cremations will be banned, this ghat sealed off, mark my words. Then we are on the streets. But if we pull this off, we are good for two-three months, right? Each of us will make forty thousand cash – counting Mishraji and Shankar's lot – over these two days. We take it and run, find refuge in some quiet village, till this storm has blown over. Or else, you will have to light my pyre or I yours, very soon.'

'But where…'

'First, let's get the money in our hands, then we can talk about that. No point oiling your moustache with the jackfruit still on the tree, is there?'

'Forty thousand…' Shibu muttered to himself.

'Yes, that too at a time like this. It's our last chance, Shibu. Remember how we used to laugh and say that if there is one profession that's recession proof, it is ours – people will never stop dying. Well, nice lesson mother nature has taught us now, ha?'

Shankar called within the hour. The family had agreed to his terms. They would wire the money as soon as he WhatsApped them a photo of the death certificates. Shankar was on his way to the doctor's house; he would withdraw money from the bank on his way back.

He would call Kallu once he had the cash with him.

'Done,' Kallu said coolly as he disconnected the call, though barely managing to suppress a smile.

Shibu clapped his hands.

'Okay, let's plan this out. You go get the bamboo stretcher from Saraswati's house. Give her some cock and bull story, and 500.'

'That much?'

'Well, she isn't getting it back. On the way back, stop over at Modna's and get the keys to his godown. Tell him there's a slim chance of receiving a body late at night; it's stuck somewhere in transit. Easy to believe. Say if it does turn up, we will take some cheap firewood and pay him for it tomorrow. Better still, give him a small advance, couple of hundred. Can you manage this?'

Shibu nodded.

'Easy. But how will we...'

'Don't strain your feeble mind; leave it to me. I have a plan. Go now. And give me Shankar's number before you leave.'

Once Shibu had left, Kallu called another number. 'Jamuna? Recognized my voice?'

There was a trill of laughter from the other side.

'Who knows, these days it is tough to say. Listen, how are things in the village? No cases,

I hope? Good. So, as you can imagine, things are not very good here. I was thinking of coming there and lying low for a few weeks. I have some money with me, so food and stuff shouldn't be a problem. No issues, I hope?'

That was settled. Jamuna was a widowed girl whose father had been a *dom* at the ghat during Kallu's father's time. Her deceased husband had a small plot of ancestral land in Amwa, where she lived with her four-year-old daughter, growing vegetables and doing odd jobs for a living. Kallu had had a scene going with her, on and off, for some time now. Everyone in the village knew, they just looked the other way, perhaps out of sympathy for the poor girl's misfortune. Like Shibu, Kallu had never married. But this was as good a time as any, he thought, for tasting the fruit of conjugal bliss, even if only for a short while. Why die with regrets?

Shibu would be left alone, but he was a tough nut. Years on this ghat, fending for himself, how could he not be?

Kallu sat on his haunches, waiting. In the distance, he could see a huddle of men smoking bidis. They would sit there the whole day, waiting for a corpse to arrive, before dispersing dejectedly as the light faded. They were competitors, in a sense, but he felt for them. It had been over a fortnight since business started dwindling. What were they eating? He stood up and walked across.

'What's up, Lakhi? Any gossip?'

'The only gossip, guru, is that this bloody lockdown won't end anytime soon. Some shops may open, but what good is that to us? Our pockets are also in lockdown…'

Lakhi was right, what option did they have? Kallu felt a sudden surge of rage, assuaged somewhat by the satisfaction of fleecing Mishraji and Shankar's advocate client – just the kind of entitled fuckers who saw to it that his lot never dared cross the line drawn for them at birth.

'Any money saved up from before, or drank through everything?'

He knew the answer to that. None of them thought beyond the day. Such was their lives, interwoven with the business of death, that the only future they could ever contemplate was the inevitable. In a way, it prepared them; yet the problem of meals remained.

'Come with me,' he said, on a whim, and led the flock to the Kashi *mithai bhandar*. For some reason, the sweet shop had been allowed to remain open throughout. Maybe the cops gave it a special concession for being such an old institution.

Durgadas, the corpulent owner of the shop, sat on a wooden bench, swiping away flies with a duster. He looked warily at the group.

Kallu addressed him, 'Durgadas, give all of them a plate of alu puris, jalebis and milk. My treat, how much?'

Durgadas stared with his mouth open.

'What happened? How much…' Kallu asked again.

'Oh, that will be 350.'

Kallu counted the money out and handed it over. The men, equally shocked, stood waiting around him.

'Go, sit down. And next time, if you are lucky enough to get a client, remember to save some of the money. You folks haven't figured out the gravity of the situation yet.'

Kallu watched as they were served. He observed two of the younger *doms* – they were brothers – with particular interest. An idea flitted across, but he shook his head and walked away before it could get a hold on him.

The day progressed smoothly for them. Bishu, the doctor, accepted his fee with such alacrity that Shankar thought he may have even done the job for less. The dead couple's son already had Shankar's account details, and the money reached minutes after he had sent them a scan of the certificates. Shankar marvelled at how canny Kallu had been, wondering, as he often had before, why the man never applied his mind to a more ambitious enterprise. He didn't lack in intelligence, or imagination; only a surname.

Shibu returned to say that the stretcher had been procured and he had the keys to the woodshed. Kallu called Shankar.

'I have your cash,' was the first thing Shankar said, on answering.

'Good. Now listen carefully. Get your boy to open the room and wrap each corpse with a clean bedsheet. Head to toe. Then use another bedsheet and do this again. Two per dead body. Clear?'

'Yes.'

'Then ask him to scrub himself with soap all over, change into new clothes. Don't you dare omit this part, because I will ask him. That's it for now. You count our money out and keep it ready. Shibu is coming for it now.'

'But…'

'Need the money in advance, or we can't go ahead. We will meet you at the ashram around eleven tonight. Ensure all the other residents are packed off to bed by then, and the boy is around to help us. Now, I have work to do.'

He gestured for Shibu to set off.

The afternoon wore on. Predictably, there were no arrivals; another day of business washed out. As the colours changed on the water, the men began to depart in small groups. The younger ones lingered, always more hopeful.

Shibu arrived with a bounce in his stride. He patted his pocket and grinned.

Kallu put his hand out.

'All of it?'

'Why, think you won't get your share?'

'No, no…'

Kallu counted the money and handed half of it back to Shibu.

'Now take a piece of soap and go wash your hands well.'

It took Shibu a second to catch on. 'You really think Shankar…'

'No one ever died from being careful.'

'Shall we get the wood then? Sorry, after dark, right?'

They waited. Suddenly, Kallu asked, 'Ever thought of doing something else?'

'Huh? Leave this work, you mean?'

'Yes. No cremations, no dead bodies, no ghat. Then what?'

'To tell you the truth, Kallu, I did think about it once. Around the time there was all this talk – remember – about cleaning the river, modernizing the ghats, installing electric crematoriums. I felt we would become redundant. But then I thought, the pace at which things happen here, by the time the Ganga gets cleaned, it will be time for our pyres to be lit anyway. Heh.'

'Think again, seriously. Sometimes, Shibu, a jolt comes with a purpose – to shake us out of our rut. You and I aren't the kind to sit and starve on the banks of the Ganga, right?'

'But, here everyone knows us as *doms*, what else can we do, Kallu?'

'You have answered your own question. It cannot be here, then. Didn't you have an uncle in Gorakhpur? Best if you can leave the state, though, where our shadows can't follow us. Start thinking, something will occur to you. There is time. No way you can travel anywhere tomorrow, even if you wanted to.'

Kallu's words alarmed Shibu. He stared morosely at his callused feet till the darkness began to gather around them.

Finally, Kallu snapped out of his reverie and said, 'Come, might as well sort the wood out in the shed and keep it ready.'

As they walked, they saw the two *dom* brothers loitering on the road. Something occurred to Shibu.

'Kallu, if you are really worried that we might pick something up from…from the ashram, why not sublet that part of the work to,' he pointed his chin towards the boys.

'Already thought about it. No, Shibu, we won't do that. This burden is ours to lift. We have been paid, now we will take the risk. Can't go about double-dealing with matters of death. It will return to bite us in the ass.'

At the woodshed, they made two separate bundles tied with ropes. Kallu fetched a can of kerosene from the corner and placed it next to the wood. They locked the door behind them and stepped out. There was still time so they decided to have a quick bite, though Kallu shot down Shibu's idea of a tipple. Not before the job, he said.

The ghats were deserted when they reached the gate of the ashram, carrying the stretcher between them. Kallu had always found the building depressing – that pall of decay hanging over it, with its old inhabitants who nobody wanted, awaiting their summons – but today it looked even more spooky. Dimly lit corridors with shabby green walls and the locked doors behind which the residents slept, carrying who knows what contagion inside them.

Kallu called out, and Shankar opened the door.

They placed the stretcher on the ground. Kallu said, 'Ask the boy to place the wrapped bodies on this, one on top of the other.'

They stepped away.

In a minute, Kanai emerged, a cloth covering his mouth, with a bundle held in front of him. Shibu was surprised at the size – how much a body shrank with age. Kanai dumped it on the stretcher like a sack of potatoes, then folded his palms in a greeting.

'Get the other one, Kanai. Fast.'

He went back and returned with another bundle which was even smaller. Kallu turned to Shankar.

'Give him his money.'

'I will…'

'Now, in front of us.'

Shankar reached inside his pocket and extracted a bundle of notes, from which he counted out a few. He handed them to Kanai, making sure their fingers didn't touch.

'Count it, Kanai,' Kallu said.

'Ten thousand,' said Kanai, looking utterly confounded.

'Right. Now listen carefully, Kanai. Get some clothes, go and have a dip in the river. And then, get the hell out of here. You are not to return for the next month at least. Go anywhere; if I see you, I'll break your legs, okay?'

Kanai nodded and ran off.

'Was that necessary?' Shankar protested feebly.

'Shibu, you take one side, I'll take the other. Wear your *gamcha* around your mouth first.'

Without another word to Shankar, they turned away and began their trudge back to the ghats, stealthy silhouettes against a dark Benaras sky. They paused at the woodshed, to toss the bundles of wood and can of kerosene on top of the bodies. The whole place was deserted, not even a stray dog in sight.

At the appointed place, where Mishraji's pyre had also been lit, they quickly made two log beds.

'Let's tip them over carefully, one in each,' said Kallu, and they managed this expertly without touching the corpses, or dismantling the pyres. Shibu sprinkled the kerosene generously, Kallu tossed the matchsticks. The fires roared. They did a quick survey of the surroundings. No one in sight, still.

'You go have a bath first. Remembered the soap bar, fresh clothes?'

Shibu stripped down to his underwear and chucked his clothes into the flames before heading down to the river. Once he was back, Kallu followed.

It took a couple of hours for the fire to burn itself out, reducing everything to a pile of ash and embers. With a stick, Kallu scattered the rubble around and Shibu poured water over it, so that in the morning, it wouldn't appear as if fresh pyres had been lit at night. Why make people curious, unnecessarily?

It was the dead of night, still some time before the first hint of light appeared on the horizon. Kallu decided to set out as soon as dawn broke; the walk to Amwa would take between four and five hours, with a tea stop in between.

Shibu had guessed his plan. 'You will leave for Amwa?'

'Yes. I want to try living differently for a while. Work on the field, grow stuff, figure out what else can be done in that village. See what these two hands are good for. Don't need much, just enough for dal roti.'

'And booze...'

'I am quitting from today. At least, I will try my best. Enough of all that, time to clean up a bit,' he added.

Shibu snorted, but Kallu's words deepened a sense of despair that had been growing in him through the evening.

He changed the subject. 'I am worried about having carried the corpses, Kallu. And the smoke, we must have inhaled that too. Do you think that might…?'

'Don't think about it. Which sickness have we not come in contact with over the years – bodies with TB, cholera, cancer, pox…all have graced our pyres. Have we ever stopped to ask? If we are still standing, then we have become immune to everything, *saala*.'

'But these bodies…'

'Shibu, they were long dead. The dead cannot hurt us, except in our dreams. It's the living we have to be careful of.'

They sat staring at the river. Even the water was still, as if in sympathy with the surroundings. Shibu suddenly had a feeling that after today, he would not see Kallu again. When the first light of day appeared and Kallu stood up and dusted his trousers, he felt certain of it.

~

2

Holidays

Achala froze when she heard the words, hoping she had misheard them. She had been dreading this since the day Jayanti, who lived in the same chawl, shared that she had lost her cleaning job at the Eves Only Beauty Parlour. She had discussed it often with Amol at night, in hushed tones, once the boys had gone to sleep.

Pretending not to have heard, she asked, 'Did you say something to me, didi?'

'I said you shouldn't come tomorrow onwards. Everyday there are new cases in our area, and it isn't safe, for you or us. Only a matter of time before the building society sends out a notice asking outsiders not to be let in. I am surprised they haven't yet.'

'Oh.' Achala dropped the broom at her feet and waited.

'It will be inconvenient, but we will just have to manage on our own. I have discussed it with sir and he agrees. Why, what are they saying at the other house you work in?'

'I stopped going there last week, didi. They said they would call when things get better,' said Achala, looking down at the floor, as if she had been caught lying.

'There. It's just pragmatic, nothing else. Don't think it's because we are afraid you will get the disease home or anything like that. You are very clean, but it can happen to anyone, right?'

Manish looked up from his laptop. 'And Achala, don't think this has any bearing on your job with us, okay? Just call and give didi your bank details – you have an account at the Canara Bank near your house, right – and your salary will be wired on the first of the month. Treat this as a paid holiday.'

Achala giggled nervously, in relief.

'Of course, that goes without saying. Didn't I mention it earlier? Stay at home, make *puran poli* for the boys, put your feet up and watch *Ramayana* on TV,' Rekha added.

When her work was done for the day, Achala walked across to where Rekha sat.

'Didi, I'll be off then. If you need anything, just give me a call.'

'Here, take this. The coming month's salary, you will need it. And keep some extra *dal-*

chawal-atta at home at all times, okay? We'll speak on the phone. Take care.'

'Thank you, didi. Bye.'

She slunk out of the house. Once the door had closed behind her, Achala shut her eyes and took a deep breath. The wad of notes was heavy on her palm. She felt a pang of guilt – people weren't that bad after all.

'No work from tomorrow. From today, my holidays have started too,' she announced to Amol and the boys on entering her room.

The boys smiled but Amol looked tense. He got up from the floor and signalled for her to walk out on to the balcony outside.

'Nothing to worry. My salary will go to the bank directly, they promised. And here.' She took the money from inside her blouse and showed it to him.

Amol's face relaxed. '*Chalo*, at least one job is safe then.'

'Why, you think the other is gone?'

'I don't trust these Gujjus. They may not have sacked you yet, but let another month pass and you'll see. They won't be able to bring themselves to count out the notes and hand them over for no work done.'

Achala didn't say anything. Maybe he was right. But right now, her bigger worry was Amol's job with the local courier service. There had been no communication from them yet, one way or the other, and she knew that Amol had misgivings.

'It's not as if the boss is a bad person or that he dislikes me, but if there is no business how long can he go on paying us, huh? Something has to come in for it to go out, no?' was what he had told her.

'At the end of the month, I will call Mehta Madam and ask. This month's salary, I am sure they won't hold back. I did work for a week after all, and what is 6,000 for them anyway?' Achala said.

'It doesn't work like that, Achala. The bigger the house, the tighter the fist. You should know that better than me, after all these years.'

Achala took the money out again and counted out 2,000. 'Here, no point waiting for Gopal Bhai to turn up at the doorstep. We have to keep repaying the instalments.'

Amol made a face.

'What a waste. Had we known this thing would happen, would we ever have taken such a big loan? Now, heaven knows when Hari's college will open again, if at all, and the fees are paid for the year. I feel like kicking myself.'

'What are you saying, Amol? Hari has to go to college, right? That's one thing we agreed never to compromise on. Besides, how could we have known that such a thing would happen? It's like a flood or an earthquake, no? I am sure the college will make some allowances once it opens.'

'Keep hoping. Meanwhile, this 2,000 a month will kill us.'

'Listen, let's not get into this now. We'll sit at night and calculate our expenses. Even after paying off the loan and rent, we have money for food. Things are hardly going to be like this forever.'

Hari came out from the room. '*Ayi*, you are making lunch today then?'

'Yes, what do you want? Shall I make alu parathas?'

'Yes, yes!' Samir's voice floated from the room.

Amol and Achala considered themselves fortunate to have a room at the sought-after CBD chawl. Unlike other chawls in the city, this one was bang in the middle of a posh South Mumbai residential area and the only one within a 10 square-mile radius. Perhaps because of this, it was well maintained and gave the impression of being a lower middle-class housing colony rather than a glorified slum. Most of the families had members working in small commercial establishments in the area or as help in residential households, and were in their own way, comfortably off. Till this thing arrived out of nowhere, disturbing the delicate equilibrium of their lives.

The alu parathas were a hit. Achala had rolled two thick ones per head but could see that the boys were not done and she gave them one of hers to share. Hari had quietly picked out a few pieces of mango pickle from the glass jar in the common balcony outside.

'Did you ask Ajji?'

'She is dozing with a handkerchief tied across her face.'

Achala gave him a playful whack on the back. Without getting up, she tugged the cylinder next to the stove. It shifted easily.

'One more week?' asked Amol.

'Maybe.'

After finishing her paratha, Achala took the utensils to the common bathroom at the end of the corridor. Surprisingly, it was unoccupied. She washed up quickly and rushed back to the room. The balcony was no more than three feet wide – these days she felt scared to pass someone on the way, especially if the person wasn't wearing a face cover, as she was always careful to. Didn't these people watch the news, she often wondered.

Amol, Hari and Samir were sprawled out on the floor. Today, Achala would join them. There was no work to be done. Usually, in the afternoons, she would go down to the tailor's shop next to the chawl and help out with the stitching. She could darn better than the master tailor. She didn't do it for the money – though Shafiq Bhai would always slip her a note before she left in the evening – but for the company. There were two other women who worked on the sewing machines and Achala liked chatting with them. But since yesterday, the shop was closed, her afternoons empty. She gave Samir a nudge with her toe, to make some space, and she lay down on the floor. It was nice and cool on her sweaty back. That was as much as the room could take in – four people lying side by side – yet they had everything they needed. The stove in one corner, TV in the other, a small used freezer box bought from the neighbourhood cold storage, two mattresses rolled up against the wall for the night. It was their tiny universe and they lacked nothing. Achala's eyelids grew heavy from the comfort of that thought.

Later in the day, after tea, Amol wanted to go for a walk but there was a police van parked right outside the chawl and he dropped the idea. The other day he had been told off by a constable, though he had stepped out only to buy milk. The man had also said something nasty. ‘Why, isn’t the wife at home? Go lie down sticking to her – this is the time to grow the family. There won’t be a better opportunity. Go!’

Achala came out of the room and ambled towards the stairs. ‘Where are you off to?’ he asked her.

‘Just downstairs, to the courtyard. Maybe I will look up Jayanti.’

Amol didn’t need to ask her to be careful; Achala wore a mask the minute she stepped outside her door and washed her hands some twenty times a day.

Achala knocked on Jayanti’s door and stepped away.

‘*Arrey*, Achala? Need something?’

‘No, just got bored of staying in the room. Thought I would come by for a chat.’

‘Good, wait let me wear the hanky and come. Else, they will start barking.’ She pointed to the cops standing by the van.

‘You found something?’ Achala asked when she returned.

‘What? Oh, are you mad? What new job can one hope for now? And who to ask? You are lucky that way. At least in homes, they won’t fire you that easily.’

'Well, we'll see how it goes. From today, I have stopped going to work. We should be fine for a month, but after that?'

'Hmm. Don't worry, they will always need someone to clean the house, right? All this sweeping and swabbing, your hoity-toity madams won't manage it for too long.'

'True. But they are also scared of getting it from us. What's worse, you say – bending your back, or lying sick?'

Jayanti nodded. There was something to what Achala said. It also struck her that these families may get into the habit of cooking and doing the housework themselves, and then the services of help like Achala wouldn't seem that indispensable. Why, only the other day she heard someone on TV saying that most people in America or London couldn't imagine employing a cook or driver. If they could do without there, why not here? But she didn't mention it. Why add to her friend's worries?

It turned out that Achala was already thinking along those lines.

'I was wondering, it must be bad for these people with office jobs too, no? Amol was saying a lot of people are being asked to leave or accept big salary cuts. If their income goes down, they will be forced to cut their monthly expenses too, right? The axe may fall on us.'

'What will come of thinking about all this, Achala? Whatever has to happen will happen. It is not in our hands. At least we have a roof over our heads, food on our plates for now. Think of those labourers we saw walking back to their villages and their predicament.'

Achala was about to head back up the stairs when she heard the sound of the police van starting. They looked at each other, not needing to say anything. As the van moved away, Jayanti tiptoed to the gate and craned her neck out – there was no cop in sight. She gestured for Achala to come across and they stepped out together.

It wasn't prudent to walk towards the main road, so they decided to take a stroll down the inside lanes. A man walked ahead of them along with a big, brown dog on a leash. On the opposite footpath, a lady in trainers marched briskly. As far as the eye could see, these were the only people in the alley – an alley where there were more people even in the dead of night, on an ordinary day. They went in the direction of the lady. It felt like an adventure.

Suddenly, a khaki-clad policeman appeared out of nowhere just as they reached the street crossing. He smiled at the lady and called out a greeting.

Achala hesitated but Jayanti said, 'Just keep a little distance, he won't stop us.'

She was wrong. The moment the cop saw them, he shouted, 'What's wrong with you? Don't you know you are not supposed to walk around? Now, don't give me that line about going to a shop. Shops have been shut for the day. Turn back and go home, right now. And I don't want to see you again on this road, understand?'

Achala muttered an apology and they walked away.

Amol stood at the chawl gate. 'You went out?'

'Yes, just to check if the *kirana* store was open. We were gone for all of two minutes, Amol Bhai,' said Jayanti before he could take off on Achala.

'Go in.' Amol grunted and followed Achala up the stairs.

Hari and Samir looked up expectantly as she entered the room.

'Shops were shut?' Samir asked.

'Yes, it's past five. Why, what did you want?'

'Nothing, thought you had gone to get something for dinner.'

'*Chalo*, if you guys agree to help, I'll make something nice. *Puran poli* or veg biryani?'

'Biryani!' Samir yelped, before Hari could get a word in.

'Okay, but *puran poli* tomorrow then, *Ayi*,' he said.

'Fine, look in the basket and see what you can find for the biryani.'

Hari rummaged through it and came up with a handful of carrots, peas, some potatoes and onions.

'That will do. Go wash the carrots and potatoes and then peel them.'

'And me?' Samir asked.

'You rinse the rice. Show me first how much.'

Achala got the pan out. She enjoyed sitting with the boys once in a while, preparing dinner. They were usually studying in the evening, but now that routine was suspended, at least they had each other's company. It was Amol who found himself at a loose end. Neither could he go out, nor stay in the room for too long. There was the television but how much of that could one watch?

He walked in and, seeing Hari bent over the carrots, said snidely, 'I see, now you are also training to become a domestic help? Nothing to study? All those fat books that you made me buy, of no use now?'

'I asked him to help.'

Amol left the room.

Once the carrots were chopped, Hari asked, '*Ayi*, did Baba say anything about his office?'

Achala shook her head.

'And your jobs?'

'Good you reminded me, pass me my phone. There, it is charging.'

Achala scrolled for a contact named 'Mehta Madam' and called. She waited for a while and kept the phone down.

'She didn't answer.'

Hari looked even more downcast. '*Ayi*, the college fees, what will happen if…'

'You don't have to worry about that. This year is paid in advance, right? We'll do something.'

'Sunil came by today, just to say hello.'

'Really? Wearing a mask, I hope? How is he doing?' Achala asked.

'Not too well. Money problems at home. His newspaper delivery job is gone; people aren't taking papers any longer.'

'Yes, that doesn't surprise me. How much was he making there?'

'Twenty-five hundred a month, but for only two hours work in the morning. His college fees come from that. You think it will start again, *Ayi*?'

'Maybe after a while, who knows? But for the delivery jobs to survive, the newspapers have to, first. Anyway, ask him not to roam around looking for jobs now.'

'Hope classes resume soon.'

Samir, who had been listening to the conversation, said, 'How will it open, Dada? Don't know about your classrooms but in my school, there's no way boys can sit even three feet apart, forget six. If one boy gets it, everyone will. How can they allow classes to resume?'

'Pass me the salt. You don't have to worry about all this now – there are smarter people in charge of deciding that. Just read a bit every day, so that you don't fall out of touch whenever school opens. And you too, Hari.'

'Yes, *Ayi*.'

'But *Ayi*, shouldn't Dada have done medical instead of engineering, you think?'

'Why?'

'Why? Because doctors will be the most in demand now, no? They will have the most important jobs, the best paid ones.'

'And cities will stop needing buildings, roads, bridges?' Hari asked.

The biryani didn't turn out as good as usual. It was a bit too soggy. They finished it off though and as the boys laid the mattresses out inside the room, Achala joined Amol on the balcony.

'I called Mehta Madam, she didn't answer. Or call back.'

'Oh.'

'Will try again tomorrow morning. You managed to speak to Shetty Sir?'

'Yes. He asked me to go over to the house on Monday. But his tone wasn't encouraging.'

Long after the lights were turned out, Achala could hear Amol fidgeting.

The next day stretched even longer. Usually, Achala would be up at six, use the toilet, make tea and wake Amol up. She set out for the Mehtas' at quarter to seven, finish there, then head to Rekha Didi's house at around nine-thirty. By the time she got back home it was noon, the house empty.

Today, her eyes opened at six, as usual, and the prospect of an entire day without anything to do seemed daunting. The boys had been home for a few days now and were slowly getting used to it. The four of them sat around with their roti-chais, making idle chit-chat, till Amol got up and switched the TV on. Achala didn't like the idea of watching telly in the mornings. For her it was an evening thing. She thought of going down to the courtyard but got hooked on to a serial, and then another. Before she knew it, two hours had passed. Finally, she shook herself out of her lazy stupor and threw a bundle of clothes into the plastic bucket by the door. In the bathroom, scrubbing and pounding them on the slimy floor, she couldn't help wondering who had been there before her, touched the tap, sat where she had, leaned against the same wall. No way of knowing who carried what bug inside them, was there? What could this flimsy mask do for her?

In the daylight, their room seemed so much smaller, as if the walls had closed in. The balcony too, became a thoroughfare in the mornings; one could barely walk without brushing against someone's elbow. There was no question of hanging around there, staring down at the courtyard, where each family took turns – to loiter, hang washed clothes on lines, even lay out red chillies or pickles to dry. It was as if each room had someone keeping watch, ready to scurry out with their things at the first sight of a gap. Theirs was a family of four, but some rooms had as many as six people in them. She wondered how they managed. Achala made a mental calculation – three storeys with 20 rooms on each floor lined across the U-shaped balcony; even if she assumed four to a room, that added up to 240 people. All at home at the same time, with nowhere to go. Her head reeled. What if even one of them…she put the thought out of her head.

The days passed slowly. It was so strange – how, on her work days, Achala would often pine for a holiday; to be able to sleep for an extra hour on Sundays like Amol and the boys, not have to walk from room to room bent at the waist, broom in hand. And now that she had all the time in the world, she felt suffocated. By the third day, it began affecting her physically. She didn't sleep nearly as well as she did earlier. How would she? To sleep you needed to be tired, though she felt a different kind of tiredness, as if rust had begun to gather on her bones. Once, she bumped into Jayanti on her way out of the toilet. She asked her, 'Anything happened?'

'What do you mean?'

'Whatever you went in to do, did it happen? I can't seem to get it out any more, you know. Just sit there and grunt but nothing happens. Everything has gone for a toss.'

It was true, though Achala was too prudish to discuss it with anyone – her bowel movements had become irregular. All that rest, which she thought would energize her, did exactly the opposite – it turned her into a listless wreck. Cook, eat, watch TV, repeat. That became her daily routine, such that even trotting down the few steps to the courtyard seemed less and less appealing as the days passed. She tried telling herself it was only for a few days but didn't believe it. Amol grew increasingly restless and Achala found ways to send him to the shop twice a day, to buy small things for their meals. She tried to spend time talking with the boys, but Hari was a college-going boy; it wasn't the age to hang with his mother, peeling vegetables. Sometimes, they heard loud voices from the rooms at night, more than the usual.

On Monday, Amol shaved in the morning and changed into his work clothes. Before the boys could get their hopes up, Achala said, 'He's going to meet Shetty Sir at his residence. The office is shut.'

As Amol was leaving, she said, 'Come back home after the meeting.'

'Why, where else do you think I will go?'

Shetty, the owner of the courier company, lived in a small apartment a mile or so away from the chawl. He didn't own the flat. His father had leased it some fifty years ago, and he still paid 30 rupees as rent. For all practical purposes, it was his. No one would ever be able to evict him.

The door to the flat was open when Amol walked up that morning. He didn't have to knock, Shetty was sitting on the bed with a cup of tea in hand. He wore a singlet, lungi, no mask.

'Ah, Amol. Come in.'

'It's okay, sir. I'll stand here and we can talk.'

'Yes, right. So, Santosh was here a few minutes ago and I'll tell you what I told him. I don't see how this business can carry on, Amol. I may be lucky with the rent on this house, but the lease on the shop is a full one lakh every month. We have no idea when business will start again, and even if it does, we don't know what fraction of our regular revenue we will be operating at. But the rent will have to be paid and salaries for the six of you. I am not a rich man, Amol. I make just enough to pay the bills, that's all.'

Amol had expected this. He said, 'Sir, I understand. But can't you take a loan for the moment, to tide over this phase? I heard they are making loans much easier to get.'

'Easy? Haha. Not for mom-and-pop shops like us. That is for the big firms; as they say, like rubbing oil on heads already slick with it.

And even if I did get a loan, I would still have to pay it back, right? From what? The stress would kill me. No, Amol, this won't work.'

'Then...'

'Then what? I have spoken to the landlord and told him I cannot pay rent. If he can wait for a few months, I will try to restart and slowly pay back the pending amount for the months the shop was shut, not immediately. I doubt he will agree. So, as of today, we don't exist, Amol. If, by some miracle, this thing goes away next week and all is well, I will do my best to pick up the pieces again.'

'Sir, I have a family to look after. What do I do?'

'I know, Amol, I know. But you tell me, what option do I have? Where will I find a couple of lakhs every month to keep this operation going? The PM says don't fire employees, but how not to? For him, it's just a nice thing to say on TV, the cheques have to come from us, no? All this is fine for the Tatas and Birlas, not minnows like us. Here, take this.'

He took out some notes from under a pillow, obviously counted and kept in advance, and tossed it on the table at the foot of the bed. At another time, Amol would have felt insulted at this gesture. But perhaps Shetty Sir only meant to minimize contact. He picked it up. He was used to handling money and didn't have to count to know it wasn't much.

'Shetty Sir, at least this month's salary if possible...'

'Amol, please don't embarrass me. The shop hasn't been open for a single day, where will I get your salaries from? I am dipping into my own pocket even for this, so that you can buy some food items. It's the best I can do. As I said, if things get better, I'll call you. I am sorry.'

There wasn't more to be said. Amol folded his palms and walked away. Outside, he counted the money, only 2,000 – in 100-rupee notes to make it look more substantial. Enough to cover next month's college loan repayment, nothing else. He felt angry, not at Shetty, but himself for not being more careful with their earnings when the going was good. Between Achala and him, they earned close to 30,000 a month. Could they not have tucked away even 5,000 into an account? How handy it would be at a time like this. But then, movies at the Regal Cinema with the family, a day at Elephanta, pizza on the first Sunday of the month, a pair of sneakers for Samir – all seemed important. What else did they have, after all, for life – in their eight by ten feet cage – to seem a little bigger than it really was?

There was about 3,000 in the steel box on the ledge of the wall where they kept their money, that was it. Other than the loan, there was the room rent, electricity and mobile bills, gas, Samir's school fees and finally, food. Amol passed the milk booth on his way back, but decided not to buy a packet. He had heard murmurs from the family about plans to make *shrikhand* at home yesterday. All that had to stop – they were in a crisis, hardly the time to be splurging on treats.

On reaching home, he saw Hari and Samir playing football in the courtyard, wearing only shorts and masks. They froze at the sight of Amol, but he ignored them and continued up the stairs.

Achala was chopping something in one corner. She looked up and asked, 'What happened?'

'Give me a glass of water.'

She poured it out. 'So?' she asked again, trying to keep the anxiety out of her voice.

Amol took the wad out of his pocket and tossed it on the floor.

Achala's eyes lit up in hope for a second, but quickly turned to disappointment the moment she picked the money up. 'You shouldn't throw money on the floor like that.'

'Really? Now I need to hear lectures from you too? Just because... And you call that money? It's like spitting in someone's face.'

Achala let it pass. She knew what must have happened, yet had to hear it from him. 'Did he say something about opening the shop after the lockdown?'

'No. He's told the landlord he can't pay the rent.'

'Oh.'

Achala looked at the two thin bangles on her wrist – they were gold. She was about to say something, but checked herself and said, instead, 'It's noon, the shops would have opened. We need some refined oil, the bottle is almost over.'

'Stop ordering me around. And I meant to tell you earlier, cut out all the parathas and biryani, okay? We have to watch how we spend now.'

'Okay, I'll go get it,' Achala said.

Amol grunted, stood up and left the room. In a minute, Achala heard some angry words floating up from the courtyard.

Lunch was a frugal affair. Samir began to complain, 'But *Ayi*, you said you will make...' but was cut short as Amol whacked him on the head.

'Shut up and eat what's on the plate. Can't you see what's going on around us? Every day some new demand, money grows on trees or what?'

He rarely raised his hand on the boys. That afternoon, they all lay down after the meal, but no one slept.

In the evening, Achala asked the boys to go down to the courtyard. She wanted to discuss money matters with Amol.

'Mehta Madam isn't answering her phone. I think it's best to plan our budget without her now. If 6,000 is all we have to manage on…'

'Four thousand,' Amol interrupted her.

'Okay, 4,000. Then we will be short.'

'You don't think I have figured that out by now?' His face was flushed.

'If there's nowhere else you could get some money from, I suggest…'

She didn't finish because the look in Amol's eyes frightened her.

'Suggest what?'

Achala slipped her bangles off and extended them towards him. 'We can sell these, or pledge and get a loan. These aren't important.'

Amol turned on her. 'Not important? These were given to you by my mother at our wedding. And now they have no value to you? I should sell these, so that you can make *puran polis* for those gluttons? Huh, huh?' He advanced menacingly towards her.

'Careful, Amol.'

'Careful? How dare you?'

He fixed Achala's jaw with a pincer-like grip in one hand and pushed her against the wall. But the shouting had reached the boys downstairs and they barged into the room.

'Baba!' Hari screamed. Amol let Achala go, stepping back. He pushed the boys aside and stormed out. Aarti Bua had run to their door from down the corridor.

'What happened, Achala?' she asked. Then seeing the tears on Achala's face, said to Hari, 'Amol raised his hand on her?'

Hari stood with his head bowed.

'Come with me, Achala.'

'It's alright, didi. I am okay. The boys are here.'

Amol returned in a while, looking contrite. He apologized to her.

'I don't know what came over me, Achala. It won't happen again, I am really sorry. Please forgive me.'

Hari and Samir offered to make dinner, but Achala rolled some chapatis and they ate in silence.

Rekha Didi called the next morning. 'Achala, how are you? All okay at home?'

'Yes, didi, you and sir are fine?'

'Yeah, we are okay. Sir was telling me this morning how I have now begun to appreciate your work, as I have to do it all myself. Haha. I thought I would call and tell you. By the time you come back, I would have become thinner and you plump, you see for yourself.'

'I have had enough, didi, of lying around. Honestly. Our bodies are used to work. This rest doesn't suit us, everything goes haywire.'

Rekha cackled and rang off.

After tea, Achala went out on to the balcony. She saw Ajji sitting on the cement platform in the courtyard, sunning herself. She was the oldest member of the chawl, and no one gathered around when she sat there. It was a way of showing respect. But she spotted Achala and beckoned her to come down. Achala went and stood a distance away from her.

'I heard something. You are alright?'

Achala nodded with a bowed head. After a while, she looked up and asked, 'Ajji, how will things be once all this is over?'

Ajji held her gaze for some time, before taking her mask off. Achala was about to tell her not to, but didn't.

'I don't know but let me tell you a story,' Ajji began. 'When I was a young girl, maybe how old your Hari is now, my father took me to Ratnagiri. He had relatives there, and there was some talk of a match for me. But the evening I arrived, there was this massive hurricane on that coast. You cannot imagine such a thing in the city. It felt like we would all perish. In the morning, when it had subsided, we went out to inspect the wreckage it had left behind. The village was almost gone. Roofs had blown off, walls caved in, giant trees uprooted, cattle lay dead, doors and windows had been shattered – I cannot describe to you what it was like. As my father and I stood speechless, the village head – an old man – came and stood next to us. I have never forgotten his words. He said, "It's only after a storm that one knows what a house is really made of."'

Ajji pulled her mask back on, leaving Achala alone with the weight of those words.

~

3

Border Town

If one had to choose a place to get stuck in, this would be it. I told myself this every morning when my eyes opened to take in the sweep of the Panchachuli – five jagged snow peaks jutting out into that breathtaking blue mountain sky. I would lie in bed – a modest cot in the cozy wooden attic of the Pangti residence – and stare, till the soft thump-thump of a little boy's footsteps on wood broke my spell. There would be a gentle tap on the door before Bhupi entered, balancing a glass of steaming tea in his tiny palms, grinning from ear to ear.

'Good morning, Greg. Here is your tea,' he would say in perfect diction. It seemed to me, increasingly, that the high point of my mornings in Munsiyari was little Bhupi's bed-tea service, more than even the grand view of the Himalaya. Bhupi was seven, the grandson of old Dhiraj Pangti – Pangtiji to everyone in the village – whose house I had been put up in. It was a private home, but the attic doubled up as a boarding house for trekkers and climbers, usually foreigners. It was an odd household, comprising the old man and his grandson; Bhupi's mother had died at childbirth and his father, Pangtiji's son, had perished in a snowstorm on a climbing expedition to the third peak of the Panchachuli range. Bhupi was only two when this happened. So, it fell to the widowed Pangtiji to bring up the little child, which he did most capably, relishing every moment of their time together.

'What is the virus doing today?' Bhupi's way of asking for the latest news on Covid-19.

'Well, why don't you tell me? Here you go,' I said, handing him my phone. Bhupi smiled shyly and shook his head. He needed me to open one of the sites up for him. Bhupi could read but wasn't fully confident about navigating the phone yet. When I first met him, I was struck by the fluency with which the boy spoke English, later realizing it was partly to do with how well his grandfather had taught him, but also because of the regular practice he got from interacting with lodgers such as me.

It was getting on to a month since I arrived in Munsiyari, having taken in many prominent state hill stations along the way over the preceding fortnight. I had been to Nepal before, but it was my first trip to India, and I intended to make the most of it. The original plan was a summer of short climbs that included the Panchachuli base camp, culminating in a trek to Kailash Mansarovar on the newly opened border road to Lipulekh Pass via Dharchula. But, by the time I made it to Pithoragarh, the country was in lockdown, and it was with some difficulty that I managed to get a jeep into Munsiyari. The hotels were shut, but a friendly man at a tea shop, on hearing I was a climber, directed me to Pangtiji's house. I arrived at his doorstep, fully expecting to be turned away – having travelled from foreign shores at a time like this – but received instead a warm welcome from the wizened old man.

'How long have you been in our hills?' was all he wanted to know of me and, on being told it was a couple of weeks at least, was satisfied that I presented no threat to his well-being.

'There's no virus here,' he said. 'If you didn't bring it on a plane, then you don't have it. You are welcome to stay here, but if you come with hopes of climbing, that won't be possible now. Not even I can organize it.'

'Which mountain did you come to climb?' asked a little boy, whose face peered out from behind Pangtiji's legs; my first encounter with Bhupi.

Hearing my reply, he shook his head and said solemnly, 'Oho, that is in China, sorry, Tibet. Not possible. You don't know about the virus?'

Pangtiji laughed loudly. I could see many of his teeth were missing.

'Meet my grandson, who knows all there is to know about these hills. Don't you, Bhupi?'

'No, you know more than me, Dada,' said Bhupi, with a grin, and suddenly I had a feeling it would be no ordeal to shack up with the two of them and enjoy a quiet vacation in this quaint little border town. Even the communication wouldn't be an issue, seeing how well both of them conversed in my tongue. I spoke a smattering of Hindi – picked up from a handbook in London and polished on my way up – but it was no match for the near perfect English that Pangtiji spoke.

That first evening, I was invited to dine with them in the kitchen downstairs. I sat on a woollen rug next to the big round *bukhari* at the centre of the room. Pangtiji handed me a glass of clear liqueur. It was smoother than a malt, with strong fruity notes, maybe of plum or apricot.

'*Chakti*,' said Pangtiji. 'It's no ordinary liqueur. A family usually has only a bottle or two, stored away for a special occasion like a marriage. Or a special guest.'

'Well, I am honoured then. And yes, the drink is special indeed.'

Bhupi sat next to the fire, the heat flushing his already rosy cheeks. He gazed at my face, not saying much. Perhaps he felt shy – it was only our first meeting. I had gathered Pangtiji was a climber from the man at the tea shop, but now that I saw his ice axe and other implements hanging on hooks on the wall, I realized he was no amateur trekker. I asked for permission and stood up to see the framed pictures on the wall. The images were of a young Pangtiji atop snow peaks. In some of them, he was standing with groups of Caucasian climbers. Had I not met him, I would have taken him for a Tibetan Sherpa.

'Were you a Sherpa, Pangtiji?' I even proceeded to ask, before realizing that it may be an insulting thing to say.

He noticed my embarrassment and said with a smile, 'Of a kind, in my younger days. Then, I attended the institute in Uttarkashi and even led a few expeditions for the border forces.'

'I am so sorry, I didn't mean it as a slight at all.'

He brushed it off. 'No shame in being a Sherpa, I would be proud calling myself that.'

There were two pictures of another Tibetan-looking man with his hand around Pangtiji's shoulders. His face lit up when I asked who it was.

'Oh, that is Dorjee Tashi. My hero, you can say, or mentor. One of the most respected names in the world of mountaineering, though he didn't get the kind of fame Tenzing or Gombu received. Everest climber, many times over. He is from Darjeeling, but was over at the Institute of Mountaineering here in Uttarakhand during my time and we became friends. We summited the Banderpoonch together – it remains my favourite climb, to this day.'

'Quite a looker too.'

'Oh yes, the girls would all swoon over him. Hasn't lost a bit of that, even in his old age. I visited him in Darj a few years ago, and he came to fetch me on a Bullet bike, wearing a black leather jacket, looking like a Hollywood star. He is an amazing guy.'

Bhupi spoke for the first time. 'He gave me a pair of his climbing gloves. There,' he pointed at a scuffed maroon pair on the wall.

'Wow, that's a prize worth keeping. So, do you want to become a mountaineer too?'

I asked this question innocently, as I didn't know then about Bhupi's father's accident. I noticed a shadow pass over the old man's face.

'No, I would not want that for him. It's too hard a life, fraught with risk. I did it because I had to, there weren't too many options for us, and I didn't want to join the army. But not him. I want Bhupi to attend a good college, have a proper career. Okay?' he asked, giving Bhupi an affectionate smile.

Bhupi nodded and said, 'But we will climb the Panchachuli together once. You promised.'

'If these old bones hold up, we will try.'

'So, you kept up with Dorjee all these years?' I asked.

'Yes, you see, there was another reason. He was extremely fond of reading. A most erudite man, unusually so for a Sherpa. And completely self-taught. A voracious reader. One evening, we were sitting around a fire outside our tents when he said, "You know, Dhiru, what gives me the greatest pleasure on my climbs? When I sit alone in the evening after a hard day's trek, thinking of something I have read recently and suddenly everything seems to hold a different meaning altogether. It's like a revelation. You should start reading, Dhiru. You know the language and you have a wonderful opportunity most folks don't. It is something to be cherished." That started me off on my own journey,' Pangtiji said, pointing to two walls lined with books.

'May I?' I asked, and he waved his hand in permission.

The titles astounded me. I had expected to see books on mountaineering and nature, but all the books were novels or plays – Dickens, Tolstoy, Chekhov, Brecht, Hardy all the way down to Bellow, Hemingway, Roth and Greene. There was even Le Carre and Wodehouse.

'This is an amazing little library you have here,' I gushed.

Pangtiji said, 'There's much more in those trunks. I have asked the owner of the book shop in Almora to get me Enid Blyton and Lewis Carroll for Bhupi. A boy should not want for books, right?'

Dinner was a soup of kidney beans, chicken stew with carrots and roughly cut home-made bread. We served ourselves from steaming pots on the stove.

'I hope this is alright. Tomorrow, we can talk about your preferences and what time you would want your evening meals. Since we don't employ any help, guests usually fetch their meals from here and return the washed plates in the morning. Would that suit you?'

I said it was absolutely fine and offered to go to the shops to run errands.

'I think you better not do that now. It may scare the locals off.'

He put it half-jokingly but I sensed there was probably a grain of truth in what he said.

'How long had you planned on being here?'

Not wishing to alarm him, I said, 'Well, the plan was to spend a few weeks here and then set off for the Tibet leg, but now it's out of my hands, isn't it? Guess I am stuck till the travel restrictions are lifted, but I won't impose on you beyond what is convenient.'

'Oh, there's no one coming here now. Stay as long as you like. We aren't used to turning away guests in a difficult situation.'

I was beginning to get used to Pangtiji's way with words, the hazy line between something said in jest, or earnest.

'Why, do your guests often overstay their welcome?'

'Not often, and they are never not welcome. I have had climbers come in with broken limbs, who have stayed for a month or longer. To be honest, I like it and so does Bhupi. It's our little window to the world outside; there's more to be gleaned from a fireside chat with a stranger than hearing the news on television. Or else we risk remaining frogs in the well.'

While we spoke, Bhupi had curled himself into a little ball and gone off to sleep, his feet tucked under Pangtiji's folded legs. It brought a smile to my lips and also a little pang of envy.

'I'll carry him to bed when I close up for the night. Don't worry, he isn't disturbed by conversation. Actually, I think he finds it comforting.'

Pangtiji showed me a picture of his son, and then told me about the incident. He asked about my life back in London. For an old, provincial man, he was very curious. We had only just met, but it felt like we had known each other for a long time. My bed in the attic was comfortable and the room smelt of cedar. It was the best I had slept in a long while.

Over the next few days, I got to know Bhupi better. I could see he had his Dada's curiosity. I would often catch him peeping at me from some corner, before vanishing into the house. One day, I asked him to come up.

He arrived, a bit tentatively, and said immediately, 'Dada says you teach at a university.'

'Yes, I do.'

'Is it shut now?'

'I guess it is because of the epidemic. But I am on sabbatical anyway. I am not expected to join before September.'

'Such a long holiday? Our school is closed too. Do you know how Panchachuli got its name, the story of the five Pandavas?'

I shook my head, though I had some idea of the Mahabharata.

'They were five brothers who made their last journey, to heaven, from these mountains. The five peaks there,' he said, turning to point at them, 'they are the *chulhas* – ovens – in which each of them cooked their last meal. That's why they are called Panchachuli, pancha means five, *chuli* is oven.'

'Wow, that's quite a story. I must write it down somewhere.'

Bhupi looked happy. Then his face turned sad and he said, 'Dada says my father is there somewhere, sleeping in the snow.'

I didn't know what to say to that.

Later that day, I told Pangtiji about my chat with Bhupi, omitting the bit about his father.

He smiled and said, 'Oh, he makes friends very easily, particularly with white men. Maybe because he sees those pictures of me standing there in the snow with them. My friends are his friends, like that, you see?'

I said I was glad to hear that; in many parts of the world I had travelled to, provincial people could be quite wary of foreigners.

'Yes, more so with every passing year, I read. But the Bhotiyas are no strangers to foreigners, thanks to these mountains. We have seen a lot of them down the years. And anyway, we were always a trading community. Till as recently as the sixties, our forefathers were nomadic traders on the salt route – Tibet and back. All the salt in these parts came from there.'

I was visited by an image of a long line of people, walking through snow, herding horses with sacks on their back.

'Just salt?'

'Mostly, but there was gold dust too, borax sometimes. In exchange for silk, jaggery, some wool. No currency involved, only barter.'

'Why did that trade stop?'

'The sixties war with China, what else? Someone sitting somewhere far away yells a war cry; a centuries-old way of life comes to a halt. In border towns like ours, there is always that risk. I still feel bad about it. Milam was such a thriving centre of trade, now reduced to a ghost town. This massive mountain wall separates the two people, but I cannot imagine there wasn't intermingling between our communities. Just look at our faces!' he broke into laughter as he said this. 'When he was younger, Bhupi would ask about his grandmother, and I would tell him she was a Chinese dancer. Haha.'

It wasn't hard for me to imagine that Pangtiji could be quite a raconteur. I never asked Pangtiji his age but guessed he would be in his mid-seventies at least, perhaps older. I had observed in Nepal that with these high-altitude dwellers, age begins to show quite early on their faces, yet you often couldn't tell if they were 65 or 80. Pangtiji was remarkably fit, as I discovered when he took me for walks to the alpine lakes of Thamri and Mehsar Kund. I was no slouch, but he always struck out a gap and had to wait for me to catch up; though he was always careful to not make me feel bad about the difference in our speed, pretending to have spotted some exotic bird or other. Expectedly, he knew every tree, bird and beast of the region. I couldn't have asked for a better guide. When our walks were over, he always brought us back home through a wooded mud path, avoiding the main market square. At first, I thought it was because these roads were more scenic, but that illusion was shattered the day the men from the village came to visit Pangtiji.

It was late afternoon and I heard raised voices in the courtyard below. From my window, I saw six men, mostly of advancing years, standing around Pangtiji, speaking animatedly. One of them pointed to the attic. I couldn't, of course, make out what they were saying, but caught the words America and Italy and began to form an impression of what the conversation may be about. Pangtiji was trying to pacify them, but he looked hassled. And then suddenly, Bhupi ran out into the courtyard and said something, and all heads turned to him. They stared down at him, but the little boy held their gaze unflinchingly. He said something else, then Pangtiji said something, and it appeared the heat of the moment had dissipated. Pangtiji patted the oldest looking man on his shoulder and walked the group out. I could see that some men were still shaking their heads, as if they were not convinced. When Pangtiji returned, I called out to him from the top of the stairs and he came up halfway.

'These guys, they have been watching the problems in the West on TV and have somehow got it into their heads that it's not safe for foreigners to enter the village. I tried explaining that you came up well before all this began, but fear is fear, there's no arguing with it.'

'Of course, I understand. So, how did it end?'

'Oh, we have Bhupi to thank for that. Just when I was struggling, he rushed out and asked,

"Do you feel scared of him? I am not afraid." They were stumped and didn't know what to say to the boy. Then Bhupi told them he sits and chats with you every day and nothing has happened to him in so many days. That saved the day.'

'Phew. But they will be back, I suspect. Maybe I should start making travel enquiries. I have been meaning to.'

Pangtiji waved his hand, as if to dismiss my concerns, but I could see he was a bit rattled. I felt bad about having put him in this position.

Later that evening, as I sat reading a book I had borrowed from Pangtiji's shelves, Bhupi came to my room. He peered tentatively from the doorway to check if he would be disturbing me, but I patted the cot and gestured for him to come and join me.

'I must thank you, Bhupi, for rescuing me from the village elders today. That was very brave of you.'

His face broke into a smile.

'If Dada went to your country, would people there be upset too?'

How did one answer such a loaded question from a child? I tried to choose my words carefully.

'Well, right now, citizens of every country are worried about people coming from outside;

it's natural to feel scared at a time like this. In any case, most airports are shut – the reason why I have not been able to go back either.'

'You will go back the day they allow you to?'

'I guess I will have to. Who knows when airports will open again. We know so little about how things will be in the near future.'

Bhupi looked glum.

'You know, they beat up a Chinese man on the road, in America. He was just walking on the road and suddenly three men ran up and started to punch him. They said he had brought the virus to America. I think if Dada was there, they may have done the same to him, no?'

I had read about similar incidents and didn't know what to say to Bhupi. Instead I asked, 'Dada must have been with you when you saw this. What did he say?'

'He said that those men were upset for other reasons – they may have lost their jobs, or seen friends fall ill – and blamed the poor Chinese man for it.'

'Yes, he is right. It's unfortunate, but that's how people often behave. Though I cannot imagine your Dada ever being attacked, he looks so calm and saintly, almost like a monk.'

'Do you think climbers from your country will stop coming to Munsiyari now?'

'Well, for some time that may be the case. With all these travel restrictions... but eventually, things will be fine again. I am quite sure of it.'

'I think people will be scared to go to any other country now. They will be scared of catching the virus themselves, or they will fear people in other countries will not want them to come, thinking they may carry it.'

I thought of presenting a more optimistic scenario but the authority with which Bhupi said these words made me fall silent.

He stood up, 'Greg, will you come for a walk to the market with me tomorrow? I want to show you something.'

His request surprised me, and before I could answer, he had run down the stairs.

I spent the rest of the evening looking up news sites for information on the repatriation of foreigners stuck in India. I even called the travel agent I had employed in Delhi. He confirmed that a limited number of flights were being organized to specific countries, the UK among them, and I should work my way down to the capital. He had all my documents and would make enquiries on my behalf. This done, I sat back and imagined how much more complicated it would have been, were I not on sabbatical, or if I had a family back in London.

The fact was that I led a very solitary life, so much so that barring a friend from the faculty, no one had even reached out to me to check how I was faring in this distant land, in the midst of all this trouble.

The next morning, I told Pangtiji about Bhupi's suggestion that I go for a walk with him.

He looked unsure, and I thought he was about to discourage me, but said, 'Well, if Bhupi has said so. The boy knows his mind.'

And so, I was ready when Bhupi turned up at my doorstep after breakfast, wearing a smart rabbit wool cap and checked scarf around his neck. Days were warm, but the mornings were still cool in Munsiyari, perched as it was so high above sea level.

Together, we walked down a sloping path, till it merged with the concrete road that led down to the main square. By now, I was familiar with the village squares in Kumaon, and while there were a few wares on display, which I hadn't seen before, the market was similar to the other ones I had seen in the region. It was still early, but the shop Bhupi took me into was open. An old lady sat sipping tea. She looked a hundred. If she was surprised to see me, she didn't show it. Bhupi pointed to some rugs rolled up on the floor and said something in their dialect. The lady got off her stool and rolled them out.

'What are these?' I asked.

'This is a *dunn*,' he said, pointing at a carpet which had distinct Tibetan flower motifs. It was thick and though not especially of fine craftsmanship, I made suitably appreciative noises. And then, she produced a simple grey blanket-like weave. Its minimalistic pattern appealed to me.

'*Thulma*. Made from sheep wool. You can use it as a blanket or even wear it around you like a shawl,' said Bhupi. He asked the woman something, before saying, 'She says it took her one full month to make it. Dada has two at home, but we only take them out when it is cold. Does it snow in England?'

'Sometimes, but not very much. But it does get cold.'

'Then you should take this back.'

I considered what this rug would add to my luggage, but decided to go for it, not having the heart to say no. Bhupi did the bargaining for me, and the lady packed the rug into a neat little bundle, which would possibly fit into my suitcase. Bhupi looked satisfied.

By the time we walked out, the market had opened and a lot of people were milling about on the main street. I could see a lot of eyes turning towards me, though there wasn't a single invitation to enter a shop and look, as I had come to expect in this country. I felt wary, but then Bhupi surprised me by putting his little fist into my hand. So we walked, hand in hand, tall white man with his little local guide, down the centre of Munsiyari village. No one said a word. I can never describe the strength his little fist gave me that day.

Pangtiji was pacing in the courtyard. He looked anxious. But when he looked at Bhupi's face and the rug in my hand, his face relaxed. Bhupi walked inside. I told Pangtiji that I would set out for Delhi soon. He didn't seem surprised.

'Today?' he asked.

'No, tomorrow morning perhaps. Guess I will have to stop at Almora for a night. Would it be difficult to get hold of a car?'

'All the way to Delhi? Hmm, let me ask around. You may have to change vehicles once. These local guys will drop you to Almora, and from there another one shouldn't be difficult to find. Expect to be stopped on the way. But with your papers you should be let through.'

I said I was expecting a confirmation for a flight out of Delhi, which would make the passage easier.

The day passed quickly, between calls to the agent and airline, packing up my few things and organizing the cab. I even spoke to an airport hotel in Delhi, in case I needed to spend a night there waiting for the flight. The errands kept me occupied, but I carried a heaviness inside all the while. Pangtiji came up and asked me to join them for a farewell dinner, but Bhupi stayed away from the attic.

The meal was an unusually quiet one, as if my imminent departure cast a shadow on it. Pangtiji tried to make conversation, saying things like, 'Maybe, once all this is over, you can return and complete the unfinished climb.'

But when I told Bhupi I would keep in touch through mail, call him sometimes, I was sure I saw Pangtiji wince.

Bhupi sat quietly next to his grandpa, looking up only once to ask, 'Did you put the *Thulma* in your bag?'

Maybe he felt it was the only thing which would remind me of him. Once again, I couldn't help thinking how wise he was for his years. I didn't sleep well that night.

The car came, as arranged, at the crack of dawn. I didn't want to linger; it was a long drive to Almora, and I had a plan to drive on to Haldwani if there was still daylight. The less I kept for the leg to Delhi, the better. I had said my goodbyes the night before and intended to slip out quietly, but when I climbed down the stairs with my bags, they were both standing in the courtyard.

'You needn't have. The car is here.'

'It's alright. I think the two of us will go for a morning walk today.'

I placed my bags in the boot and shook hands with Pangtiji and thanked him for everything. In my heart, I hoped we would meet again, though I knew how slim the chances were. From London, Munsiyari was really the other end of the world. I shook Bhupi's hand too.

He said in a formal tone, averting his eyes, 'Bye, Greg. Have a safe journey.'

I got into the car and we drove away. When I turned to wave from the corner of the road, I saw Pangtiji standing there with a smile but Bhupi had buried his face into his Dada's legs.

We drove down the winding roads, past alpine meadows and tall deodar trees, past the waterfall at Birthi till the snaking turquoise river appeared in the valley below. All the while I was visited with memories of the weeks gone by, the unlikely friends I had made in this border town. At times, I could almost feel the warmth of Bhupi's little fist in my palm.

4

The Party

Tania laughed out loudly when I told her.

'You are joking, right?'

I showed her Rahul's message. She looked incredulous.

'Have they lost it completely? I mean, what is he thinking…' she blurted out in exasperation. Tania had never liked Rahul much. He was too flamboyant for her taste. Couldn't say I did either, but that didn't come in the way of enjoying an occasional boozy evening at his pad.

I shrugged. She was right, of course. Who could even think of throwing a terrace party at a time like this? Yet, I couldn't deny that I was interested. The prospect of being around people after such a long time, sharing a drink, having a few laughs together – seemed attractive.

Tania was on it in a flash. 'Ah, I see you are tempted.'

'No, it's not that. What's the big deal in another of those parties, you know what to expect. Just that…'

'Just that you are feeling stifled, stuck with me in this house for weeks on end. Say it.'

I turned my palms upward.

'See, that's the problem. Why does it have to be a you versus me situation? It's a harmless invite to a party for heaven's sake!'

Tania looked out of the window. The terrace in question belonged to the row house adjacent to our apartment. A row of potted palms provided a natural curtain against prying eyes but when Rahul's parties were in swing, we could hear the music wafting out, even catch glimpses of guests walking around with champagne flutes. Having attended a few, I could vouch that they looked more attractive from a distance, than they were up close.

I changed the subject. There was no point getting into a silly argument over this. Now this was something I was getting better at – spotting an issue which threatened to balloon into something ugly and scotching it right there. It was the only way to survive these bouts of testiness that inevitably erupted every now and then – the venting of our frustration at this house arrest.

Just when I had steered my wife to a cheerful discussion on where we would use our Airbnb credit from the recently cancelled booking for our next vacation, the topic of the party reared its head again. Rahul's wife Simi called Tania. I knew it was Simi the moment Tania looked up from her phone – she liked Simi even less than her husband.

'Now I am invited. Yay.'

'We don't have to go. Just say no, end of story.'

Before she could retort, my phone rang. It was Rahul.

'Dude, hear me out first,' he began. 'It's not what you think. No one from outside our complex is invited. Just the Noronhas, Ronnie and Pixy, Madhav, and you two. That's it. None of them have been outside the complex gate this last month.'

'It's not that, Rahul…' I was going to say that the issue of safety hadn't even crossed my mind, and make up another excuse, when he butted in.

'Look, even mom is joining us. If anyone ought to feel shaky, it's her, right? It's really like a family gathering. You aren't walking around wearing masks at home, are you? Then? Come, it will be nice. Simi raises a glass to her friends on Zoom in the evening, but that shit doesn't work for me. So, see you around eight, okay?'

He disconnected without giving me a chance to accept or decline.

Tania asked who the other guests would be. I told her. She shook her head and walked into the kitchen.

As luck would have it, when she came out a little while later, I was standing by the window, looking out in the general direction of the row houses.

'Now stop moping like a schoolboy and tell your friend you will be there. I don't think there's anything to worry about; if there was a case in this place, the entire AIIMS staff would be in attendance.'

'*I* will be there? You won't come?'

'Nope. It will become a boy's gathering after the first drink. I'll just get stuck with Simi and her mum-in-law. So fix me a G&T before you leave, and I'll curl up and watch Mrs America on telly. Not your thing, anyway.'

I tried not to show my satisfaction at this outcome. I always liked Tania to accompany me to parties but not to the Khanna's. Rahul's gatherings degenerated, as she had described, into piss-ups. And Tania's presence, with her judging eyes and aura of disapproval, acted like a harness, constantly pulling me back from the edge of abandon. I could always tell she was filing away titbits to bring up later, to prove to me that I wasn't essentially very different from those other braggarts. There was another reason I didn't want her to come – sometimes she could be impatient with the hostess, and though Simi wasn't the sharpest tool in the box, she always recognized a put down.

'Drop in for a drink at least and then come away – it's right next door,' I offered, to make her feel like I wanted her there. But she knew me too well.

'Just go.'

I didn't push it any further and quietly typed out a message for Rahul. For the rest of the day, I sort of stayed out of Tania's way, pretending to work in the study. I peered into the bedroom wardrobe when she wasn't around, to select something for the evening. Nothing too nice, as that would invite a barb, just cool and casual. I chose linen; we would be outdoors and the evenings weren't pleasant any longer.

At eight, I fixed Tania a stiff drink, remembering to add a dash of bitters and an orange peel. I asked her not to wait up for me.

'Of course not, have fun.' If there was sarcasm in her tone, I didn't detect it. Stepping out on to the paved pathway outside our block, I felt my spirits lift. A party after what, six weeks?

It was all deserted – the patches of manicured lawn, the badminton courts, the walking tracks.

In one corner, I saw a maid sitting on the bench with a fat labrador; she stood up the moment she spotted me and I looked away so that she didn't feel flustered. It was an odd complex. There were two lines of row houses, interspersed with four blocks of low-rise condos. The flats weren't cheap, but the row houses were obviously more expensive – the guards at the gate therefore more effusive in their greetings to inhabitants of the latter.

I walked up the four steps to the entrance of Rahul's place, tucked my face mask into my pocket and rang the bell, wondering whether a simple hello from a distance would suffice, or if a handshake was expected. The door flew open and Simi rushed out cooing – clasping my shoulders, she placed her cheek next to mine.

I must have seemed rigid, as she pulled away and trilled to Rahul, who had arrived by her side, 'Haha, your friend won't even return my hug, baby! Just look at him.'

I tried protesting, but they had a good laugh over it. Rahul put a hand around my waist and escorted me inside. Reema, their leggy daughter, model-like with her straightened hair and spaghetti straps, shimmied past with a, 'Hey, Sandy uncle, how's it going?'

Rahul let out a low whistle.

'Man, don't ask how I managed to get her back from the US. Last flight out, before the shutters came down. It was touch and go.'

'Don't mention it, you will scare him away. From the States, the valley of death,' Simi ribbed.

'Oh, come on, baby, don't get after him now. Sandy, it's been a month since she came back. And with that glow on her face, I dare anyone to say she is anything but bursting with health. Age, Sandy, age. Nothing touches them.'

In the drawing room, Madhav sat, engaged in animated conversation with Rahul's mother, a tumbler of whisky in hand. I interrupted.

'Namaste, Mrs Khanna, how are you keeping?'

'Oh, Sandy. You know, no one else calls me that. Can't you say "aunty" or something like that?'

'Sure, hello then aunty. Hi, Mads.'

Madhav waved at me, effortlessly dapper as always. He lived in the row house next door and headed an online education start-up. I liked him; he wasn't like the other men in the colony. I would have seen more of him too, had he not been divorced with a reputation of being a ladies' man. Once or twice, I had caught him looking at Tania with some interest in his eyes.

Mrs Khanna was saying, 'Yes, so Madhav, to answer your question, what is so different now? Look at this place we live in – neither city, nor village; chain-snatchers and molesters roaming outside the gate. So, what do we do? Leave our gates only in cars and limit all interaction with the outside world to the bare essential, *bas*. Just think of the car as a mask and you will get my point. All we have to do is continue as is.'

'Erect more walls, you mean?'

She looked at Madhav as if he had said something daft.

A good time to intervene, I thought.

'Aunty, don't you need a refill?'

Mrs Khanna held her glass out to me.

'Thanks, beta. The Blue Label please, none of those fancy malts. Never understood what that fuss was all about. Soda and ice.'

'Small or large, aunty?'

She smiled in a coquettish way and said, 'A small drink, Sandy, what's that? Haha. Come, let's go upstairs.'

With that, she rose and we trooped up the stairs behind her.

The terrace looked swell. A table had been laid out with canapes – loads of them. There were also two drinks trollies, one with the wines and spirits, the other with mixers and ice buckets.

'Tania isn't coming?' asked Madhav.

'No, she wasn't feeling up to it. How's work?'

'Oh, never been busier. Shouldn't be saying it, but this shit is very good for our business. Hey, what are you drinking?'

I looked at the trolley. I was about to plump for a whisky when Rahul came by with a glass of champagne.

'Do you have enough of that?' I asked, giving him a chance to brag.

'Sandy, my man. Call you home and run out of bubbly? You know me better than that, buddy,' he said, pouring me a glass. 'Drink till you drop, the bar will hold.'

I raised my glass to that. It was top stuff. I felt a bit bad for Tania, at home alone nursing her gin.

The door must have been open downstairs, as Ronnie and Pixy appeared suddenly at the head of the stairway.

Ronnie looked like he had just gotten out of bed, in a pair of green bermudas, his grey hair dishevelled. He patted his protruding belly and said, 'Someone give me a drink, quickly. Aah, so good to get out, feels like I am in heaven!'

They lived in the last of the row houses on the lane. Ronnie owned some business, I kept forgetting what, and Pixy was a writer of popular Parsi cookbooks and a mean cook herself.

Ronnie took a large gulp of his drink, looked around and said, 'No music?'

Rahul appeared hesitant.

'I was thinking, Ronnie, perhaps we keep this one quiet. May not be appreciated. These days everyone is a bit jumpy, know what I mean?'

'Exactly. It's sensible,' said Pixy.

Ronnie's eyes fell on the drinks trolley.

'Wow, where are you getting all this stuff from, Rahul? We are down to the last couple of bottles at home; in fact, Pixy and I were thinking of keeping it to a single drink in the evening, to make it last. But you…'

Rahul could barely conceal his glee.

'Well, my bootlegger has stood by me in this hour of need, God bless him. For the small matter of a three-times mark up, he will deliver whatever you need. I'll give you his number, no worries.'

'Three times!' Ronnie exclaimed, surveying the bottles, as if making a quick calculation of the price Rahul was paying.

'Dude, what will you do with all your money? Drink the best stuff while you still can; what can we say about the future? Look at what's going on.'

'Money? What are you talking about? Listen, why don't I send you this month's statement of accounts, huh? It will make your eyes water.'

Mrs Khanna walked up. 'Pixy, is your cook problem sorted out, or are you still doing all the meals yourself?'

'Where, aunty? She's gone. It's me slaving away, to feed my man's voracious appetite.'

'Don't put it like that, Pixy. It stirs something in me,' Madhav said with a wicked gleam in his eye.

'Bastard, stop flirting with my wife. Find a chick for yourself,' Ronnie said good-naturedly, clapping him on the back.

Reema made an appearance, all eyes turning to her instantly.

'Dad, is there any beer going?'

'Of course, sweetie. There, in the fridge inside. Go get one.'

'Why, where's Nandu?'

'In the kitchen, getting some stuff ready. He'll be up now,' said Simi. 'Wait, let me get you one.'

'How are you coping with house arrest, darling?' Pixy asked Reema.

She made a face. 'I need a vacation, like so badly, aunty. Just go lie down on a beach bed, not have to come indoors, for a month at least,' she giggled.

'I know. It is hard, especially for young people like you. This is your time to be out in the world. Fingers crossed, hopefully it will be over soon.'

Reema took a sip of her beer, before walking away with a bored expression on her face.

The champagne was going down nicely; I had the distinct impression of watching a play in which all the actors were personally known to me.

A bell chimed – the Noronhas, I thought. Ajay, the hotelier, and his gallerist wife, Madhu. My eyes darted up towards the lit window of our apartment; I wondered if Tania might be peering down, if only out of curiosity. Of all the people gathered there, she disliked Ajay and Madhu the most. They were just the kind of people she wanted to avoid once we had decided to move to this colony.

I turned towards Madhav next; maybe it was the light but I thought I detected a slight sneer on his face. There was a history of unpleasantness between him and the Noronhas.

'The restroom is downstairs, right?' I asked Madhav.

'Yeah. The door right in front of the landing, if I am not mistaken. Going? Think I will come along too.'

At the landing, I heard voices and approaching steps, and asked Madhav to use the loo first.

It was the Noronhas, as I had guessed. Ajay clapped me on the shoulder with a breezy greeting before continuing up to the terrace.

On our way up, Madhav paused to peer at the frames on the staircase wall. Stylishly framed black and white photographs, all of Simi. Posing on a beach, wearing a sun hat, carrying a pup, raising a champagne flute, blowing a kiss. There were no less than twenty pictures of her, though of varying vintage. On the adjacent wall, the entire family was represented – Simi and Reema together, Rahul with them, hugging, kissing, huddling. Images of love and harmony, if somewhat trite, even contrived.

'Ever wondered why people living together would also want their own pictures strewn all over the house? I don't get it.'

'Different folks, different strokes, Mads. What's it to us?'

'Ah, that immortal line, explaining everything that baffles us in people. I find this self-absorption a bit annoying, frankly.'

This was Madhav's problem – judging all the time, every trivial matter. I agreed with his perspective, most times, but didn't share his impatience. I just hoped he wouldn't bring it up with Simi right away, which – knowing him – was a distinct possibility. But we reached the terrace to find all of them waiting, glasses in hand.

Since all of us had arrived, Rahul proposed a toast.

'To the end of confinement and being together again.'

We raised our glasses. It was a fine enough sentiment to clink on, but I knew someone would make a snarky comment. Sure enough, Ronnie did.

'Wish it was, my friend. But left to these jokers, they will keep us shut inside till the country is finished. With the curve, we will also be flattened for good.'

'I swear, Ronnie. Can you believe this lunacy?' said Ajay, sounding genuinely exasperated.

Madhav, the contrarian, stirred in his corner. 'So, you would throw it all open now? Business as usual?'

I could see that just for a moment, Ajay mistook this as an endorsement of his outrage, but the challenge in Madhav's tone wasn't entirely lost on him.

He answered, less assertively than he had spoken earlier, 'Well, I don't see the point of the current approach, frankly. The numbers go up every day, so what are we achieving by keeping everything closed? It's like rubbing salt on wounds.'

'Come on, Mads, people have to eat too. I mean think of ordinary people – the *presswallahs*, vegetable vendors, auto drivers – we have just snatched away their livelihoods, without offering anything in return!' Rahul added.

'And it is the plight of those people that sparks your outrage, is it?' Madhav asked, his voice still level. He was beginning to enjoy himself, I could see.

Simi looked nervous. She said, 'Oh, we do realize how lucky we are, compared to them. I told Rahul the day we had to shell out that obscene amount for Reema's ticket, how privileged we are. Most folks would never have managed.' Her eyes scanned the terrace to see if Reema had left.

Ajay kept his glass down, a bit more heavily than he ought to have.

'You know, I am getting a bit tired of this privilege shit. It's become like a standard disclaimer these days – say anything, follow it up with a "but we shouldn't be complaining". Why? I don't understand this guilt trip about being better off. It's not as if we are the ones who have denied them the right to work or snatched everything away. It's absurd!'

He turned to Rahul and Ronnie, quarters he presumably expected support from. Madhu spoke up.

'I agree. It's tough even for us. Not as bad as the poor migrants or labourers, but that was never our life anyway. We cannot suddenly start using that as a benchmark for ourselves, can we?'

I tried to steer them away from this spirited defense of their privilege, fearing a scathing attack from Madhav.

'But Ronnie, don't you worry that with the way cases are building up, we may be at the tip of an explosion? Say you open your factory, cases crop up there and you have to shut operations again, wouldn't that be worse?'

'Worse how, Sandy? It's zero now, will become zero again. But I see the risk you are talking about. It gives me nightmares. Just that this idea of sitting and waiting, losing so much business is difficult to digest.'

'Your workers are still here, or have they gone back?' Mrs Khanna asked.

'Some have left, the locals are still around. I could start with them, wait for the others to come back. Hope they do…'

'Oh, I wouldn't worry about that, Ronnie. They have to. Once they have rested a few days, the question of earning a living will rear up again. Then…' Ajay didn't finish.

'Baby, shouldn't I tell them about our collection drive for the migrants in our area?' Simi asked Rahul.

'Of course…'

'What's this, Simi?' asked Madhu.

'You know, I have been thinking for some time that we should do something for these poor guys who are walking hundreds of miles to get back home. If we pooled a kitty together for even the ones stuck at our border, that would be something, right? I know we are not the government or anything, but every little bit helps.'

'Sure, but how do you want to go about it?' I asked.

'Well, there is this outfit I know which is providing food for them every day. If a dozen of us in this complex could contribute maybe 10-15,000 each and collect one to two lakhs, that would be a reasonable amount to hand over, at least to start with.'

Rahul put his hand up. 'I am in. The first 15 from my side, Simi. Done.'

'Sure thing. Count me in too,' said Ajay.

There were nods from Ronnie and Pixy. I smiled vaguely as well, to convey it was a great idea. Though I could see Tania scoffing when I told her; even making a snide remark about how each purse of Simi's cost more than the combined kitty she was aiming to collect.

'And a contribution of 10-15,000 will make you feel better, Simi?' Madhav asked. I didn't like the look in his eyes.

'Come on, Mads. It's not nothing.'

'No, it isn't. I am just reminded of – from each according to his ability, to each according to his need.'

'I didn't know you were a fan of Marx,' Ajay said sarcastically, and I knew it was a grievous mistake, like prodding a snake with a stick.

'Oh, he was a genius, I think. Flawed, yes, his followers even more so, but that doesn't take away from the fact that he saw through the rot in all of us. And Ajay, what I am not a fan of are these pitiful attempts at salving your conscience.'

'Madhav...' I said. But he stopped me with a gesture of his hand.

'No, Sandy, let me finish. I've been thinking about this. We have all heard stories from our grandparents about the great wars – and aunty can tell us about the Partition too – but in our own lives we have not seen suffering on this scale, right? So, I say that our compassion, if it exists, must match up – we have to partake of our wealth till it pinches us, or it means nothing. Else, it is like tossing a few coins into a beggar's bowl and turning away.'

'What do you mean?' Ronnie asked.

'You guys understand numbers. Say you are worth 50 crores – please don't feel insulted, it's only an example – and you give away five to these people who have nothing. Ten percent of your wealth, which you will earn back again in a year, max two. But it won't be as easy to give away, as say Simi's 10,000. What is ever serious, if it doesn't cause the slightest discomfort, ha? Well, are you up for it?'

'Five crores, at a time like this? Are you mad?' Ronnie rolled his eyes. Luckily his jovial tone could never offend anyone.

'Ah, there you go. You say, at a time like this, Ronnie, yet you forget – to each according to his need. You stand here, sipping the finest scotch, she doesn't have a roti to feed her hungry child.'

Now Madhav sounded truly dramatic, a bit over the top even, though arresting to watch.

I glanced at Ajay – he stared at his drink, as if it were hemlock in a glass. He looked up and said, 'Madhav, in your eloquence you forget that we pay taxes for exactly this reason. And let me remind you, the rate is 44 per cent for all of us here; nearly half of what we earn is already taken away by the government for doing precisely all this! On top of that, we should pay more?'

Madhav smiled. This was when he was at his most dangerous.

'I am glad the gloves are off. The taxpayer argument, finally, to fall back on. Yes, Ajay, technically you have done your bit, by being an honest taxpayer. But we are not talking about hauling you off to jail for not helping migrants; we are talking about human compassion. Your wealth is yours, earned the fair way – I hope so – and no one is entitled to it. But how would you feel if you looked down now from the terrace and saw a line of people sitting on the streets, without a meal for the last two days, no place for shelter, no way to earn money or go back home? Would it feel right to turn away, say it's okay, I paid my taxes?'

For once, Ajay didn't snap back.

Madhav continued, 'Yet none of us can do it. Forget five crores, we would cry murder if the government were to announce a small wealth tax for people like us.'

'Jesus Christ...' I heard Rahul mutter under his breath.

'I know, Rahul, how much that idea riles you, and call me a Marxist or anything you like, but I think we need this sort of tax. Just for this year, everyone above a certain wealth bracket, pays a two per cent wealth tax. The collected amount is transferred to the bank accounts of the poorest households. No leakage. From our pockets to theirs, how about that? Next year, if all is well again, the tax is gone.'

I found myself nodding. It seemed fair enough.

The argument may have gathered momentum, but Mrs Khanna barged in with an innocuous question. 'Let all this be, Madhav. Tell me what's happening with my bank stocks, beta? I thought they were the safest, but they have tanked the most!'

I turned away to stifle a grin at the artless way in which the old lady had unwittingly defused the gathering tension.

Madhav looked like he had been punched in the gut, but smiled and said, 'Yes, aunty, even my portfolio is bleeding. This year will be bad for the banks. But, the good ones will bounce back…'

'You tell me when is a good time, alright? I just want to get rid of them when the prices recover, put it all in gold. Rahul says gold will do well now.'

'He is probably right.'

An air of relief rippled across the terrace. The moment had passed. Madhav seemed deflated, everyone else relieved. I guided Ajay by the elbow to a corner, away from where Madhav stood.

'Ajay, let it be. Madhav means well, you know that.'

'It isn't the first time, Sandy. Besides, why does he think he is the only one with a bleeding heart? Just because his business is doing well…'

This came as a surprise, as I couldn't see what it had to do with Madhav's line of reasoning. Madhu and Pixy joined us, and I offered to refill their glasses. When I passed by Madhav, he looked at me with reproach, as if I had betrayed him.

I returned to our small group to hear Pixy ask, 'Madhu, how is the art market holding up?'

'I thought it would collapse completely, but the auctions are doing fine. There is interest if you float a good piece online.'

'The guys with moolah, all stuck at home, guess that's what they are left with – punt on stocks or dabble in art,' I offered. Madhu wagged a finger at me in agreement.

She fished her phone out and sneakily showed me an image of one of those Krishen Khanna Bandwallahs.

'What do you think?'

I didn't want to sound too dismissive, in case the painting belonged to her, but I couldn't lie either.

'It's okay. I am not a big fan of these, actually. Like Hussain's horses, this does nothing for me. Sorry.'

'You don't have to be,' she said. And then in a low whisper, 'Just be ready to see it next time you come here.'

I raised an eyebrow.

'Yup, Rahul bagged it for 40 lakhs, in last Friday's sale. A birthday gift for Simi; apparently she adores them. He called to consult me when the bidding was on, don't think madam knows yet.'

I was glad Madhav wasn't within earshot.

Nandu was hovering around the trolleys. I walked up to him. We were a distance away from everyone else, so I asked, in a low voice, 'How are things back in your village, Nandu?'

I remembered that he came from Bettiah in Bihar, near the Nepal border.

'Very bad, *saab*. No income, and half the families have someone stuck in the city, unable to return.'

'They are organizing trains, so the matter should be resolved soon. At least, that will be some relief.'

Nandu shook his head. 'No, *saab*, that is a bigger worry. So far, at least the disease hasn't spread there, but now if these guys return, who knows what will happen? Didn't you hear, Didi is refusing to let the worker trains enter Bengal?'

I didn't know what to say to him. I couldn't offer help, lest Rahul and Simi take offence. Madhav joined us, but Nandu slunk away as soon as he did, casting a nervous glance in Rahul's direction.

'Was I too aggressive?'

'Can you ever make a point subtly, Mads?' I said with a smile.

'It's just that this habit of throwing crumbs and feeling smug about it bothers me. Between us, I am going to walk the talk this time, Sandy. Have got the liquidity in place, just figuring out the right vehicle. None of this PM Cares fund and all, I want the money to go straight into these people's hands. They can decide what to do with it. Will crack it soon.'

'That's good to hear, Mads. But everyone doesn't see it your way. And we are here for a few drinks and a laugh. Why mess it up?'

'You are probably right,' he said with a sigh. 'Besides... Anyway, forget it now.'

'No, go on. What were you going to say?'

'Only that, if you presented it in a less accusing tone, I feel they would consider your view more seriously; even surprise you sometimes by agreeing with what you said. Wouldn't that be even better than winning the argument?'

Madhav stared down at the ground, thinking about what I had just said. Then, surprising me, he walked over to where Ajay and Rahul stood. I saw him link his arms with Ajay and Rahul's and say something with a smile on his face. Whatever he said seemed to work, as they all broke into laughter, and Ajay even put an arm around Madhav's shoulder. Fences had been mended. The play was nearing an end, only the feast remained.

It was an incredible dinner, even by the high standards of the Khanna household. All the things that Tania and I had missed eating over the last few weeks were on the table, and I felt really bad that she wasn't there. At the door, we shook hands cordially, promising to meet again soon. If there was any remnant of the rancour from earlier in the evening, it was hidden away well. Besides, everyone was quite tipsy. Madhav left with a dejected look on his face; I couldn't say on what account.

It was past midnight; a gentle breeze was blowing, and I decided to take a stroll around the compound. Madhav's words, about being able to give till it pinched, sloshed uneasily in my head, as did the fumes from the parting shot of brandy Rahul had forced on me.

Turning the bend, I was surprised to see a couple sitting on a bench, in a dark corner next to the overgrown crepe jasmine bush. The boy was one of the night guards, I had seen his face before; the girl was probably a live-in maid. Even from a distance, I could see the girl was crying, the boy trying to console her. I turned and walked back, not wishing to disturb them. Who knew what private griefs they nursed in their young hearts?

~

5

Essential Items

The doorbell rang exactly at 11, as promised. Both of them jumped in their seats, having almost forgotten its insistent clang. It hadn't rung for over a fortnight now, and not a day passed without them marveling at how quiet the flat had become. If only the peace had come at a better time.

Meera put out a hand – for Roshan to remain seated – and hobbled across to the door. She opened it a crack and peered out. A young woman stood outside, brown paper bag in hand, a yellow mask covering most of her face, though not the smile in her eyes.

'Hello, ma'am. I am Priti, from Helping Hand. Your medicines.'

She extended the bag, taking care not to come any closer.

'Ah. Thank you so much, Priti. Don't know what we would have done without you,' said Meera, through her own mask, a green one. She added, lowering her voice, 'You see, my husband has...is not well. We tried ordering online, but there seems to be some problem with the delivery boys. Unfortunately, these are essential medicines... But then my daughter wrote to me about your service. God bless you all.'

'It's the least we can do, ma'am. Such a difficult time for everyone, more so for...'

She didn't finish. She didn't need to.

'Well, you must have many such errands to run. I won't keep you. The bill?'

'It's in the bag, ma'am. And two of the medicines weren't available.'

'Oh?'

'Thought I would give you these for now, then try and source them at another chemist's. I will come back with those, is that okay?'

'Of course, of course. But so much trouble for you...'

'Not at all. I live in Kamani house, just down the road. No trouble at all.'

'Oh, Kamani house. My friend Rajvi lives there. Do you know her?'

'Of course! Who doesn't know Rajvi aunty? She makes the best *dhoklas*, this part of town.'

'Right. Let me get you the money then. Will you come in, or...'

'I'll wait here, ma'am. It's alright.'

Meera walked back inside to fetch the money. She had kept some ready on the coffee table. She checked the bag to see which of the medicines were missing.

'Here you are. No, don't give me the change. If you do manage to find the other medicines, perhaps you can return the rest of the money then? I really wouldn't have troubled you, but one of the medicines is quite important. Roshan needs to have it every day.'

'Of course. I'll come back this evening or latest tomorrow morning. And I have messaged you my number. Please save it. You can call me anytime. Bye aunty. Stay safe.'

'You too, dear. Thank you again.'

With that, Priti was off, bouncing down the stairs.

'Here.' Roshan held out the sanitizer.

Meera took it and rubbed some on her hands. She took the mask off. Her face glistened with sweat.

'God, these masks, feels like your face is on fire.'

'I swear. Thankfully, I haven't had to wear one since Jaya stopped coming. Now who knows when we will see her again.'

'Well, she cannot come, you know that. It isn't as if she is bunking.'

'No, no, who said that? Even after this damn lockdown is over, I am not sure how long it will take for *us* to feel confident enough to ask her to resume work.'

Meera sighed. 'Well, the germ seems to have taken a special shine to us oldies. You should have seen the girl who just came by. Without a care in the world.'

'Good for her. And you shouldn't be complaining, should you?'

'True. How nice of them, really. I wish I could have given her a piece of cake at least.'

This invited a chuckle from Roshan.

Meera looked at him. Every day, he seemed to sink an inch deeper into that armchair. Despite her exhortations, Roshan had grown increasingly resistant to the idea of getting out of his chair and walking around the flat to exercise. All he managed to do was to somehow get out of bed in the morning, wash his face and lumber across to the chair by the window. There he remained all day, dozing or reading or pecking away from the snack bowls Meera would hand him. Most of the time he stared out the window. Sometimes, gazing at the trees, he would sigh and murmur, 'Who would imagine?'

She didn't know how much longer he would have the energy to even get out of bed. These days she just let him be. A thick white stubble lined his grey face, his eyes were like washed-out yolks. Sometimes, Meera would catch him staring at her. Those were the only times he looked worried.

'I hope the end comes in this house with you around. Would hate to die strapped up to a ventilator,' he had told her a few days ago, in a matter-of-fact way, as if he were expressing the need for a haircut.

Meera stacked the medicines neatly in the small wooden filing cabinet where she usually kept them. The box, an old one, had filled up slowly over time. Some new ailment or other seemed to alight on one of them every passing year. The sight of the box made her gloomy, though she couldn't deny it was those little pills which kept them going. Maybe there would be one for the virus soon, if they were lucky; another strip added to the box.

She closed the lid and went into the kitchen. It was time to prepare lunch. Since Jaya stopped coming, meals had become very simple affairs, by necessity. At 80, she didn't have the energy to rustle up elaborate dishes for the two of them, and anyway Roshan hardly ate much these days. A piece of toast, some milk, a bowl of cottage cheese, some fruit, spread out across the day – that was all he could take in, though he still enjoyed his small square of dark chocolate. It was the one sight which gave Meera hope – Roshan's eyes closing in satisfaction as he savoured this treat. On most days, she tossed some vegetables, rice and dal into the cooker and made a form of *khichdi*. That, and some curd to go with it. Of course, there were concessions, like the cake she had baked yesterday, almost in protest against this imposed frugality. A faint whiff of orange oil still lingered in the kitchen. It lifted her mood.

She opened the fridge and took out some beans, carrots and peas. The vegetable rack now looked quite empty. She put a carrot back. Jaya had brought over a large bag of fresh fruit and vegetables a few days ago and left it at the gate with the guard. But, over the last four days, the number of cases in their neighbourhood had shot up – they were now officially in a hotspot – and Meera doubted whether Jaya would drop by again. It wasn't fair to expect her to. Meera would look up the online grocery sites. She liked her vegetables off the cart, but now there weren't many other options.

'Why are you pottering around in the kitchen? Come and sit here,' Roshan called out.

He didn't like the idea of her cooking, maybe because he couldn't help. Of late, he liked her to sit close, so that he could sense her presence even if he dozed off.

When Meera walked into the sitting room, he said, 'Just boil some eggs and keep them ready. There's enough bread. I can see there are apples, oranges, so many cartons of milk. Can't we manage with all that for now?'

Meera smiled. 'We are, Roshan, if you haven't noticed. But how long can we keep eating out of packets? It's not as if this will be over next week.'

She didn't like how that sounded. 'This may last a while, I mean. We need to have fresh foods too,' she quickly added.

They sat quietly. The days were getting hotter. Outside, the yellow copper pods were in full bloom, almost perverse in their resplendence; they had not seen such clear skies in the city for years. The air was clean, streets empty, the incessant honking gone, replaced by the shadow of a pestilence that loomed over everything. In their room, they waited.

At six every evening, they took their places in front of the computer where Maya's face came alive, all the way from Manhattan. That city was going through its own version of hell, and they implored her to stay indoors, knowing how much she disliked being cooped up. It was Maya who had told them about Helping Hand after the medicine delivery guys didn't turn up. Today, they would be able to report to her that they had used the service. Roshan fell quiet every time after they spoke to her. Meera would offer him a piece of chocolate; sometimes he feigned a smile, often not.

They had just finished talking to her when the doorbell rang again. Roshan looked surprised.

'Must be Priti, with the rest of the pills,' Meera said as she went to answer the door. Sure enough, there Priti stood, with a small paper packet in hand.

'Got them, ma'am. I have put the bill and the change in the packet.'

'What a relief. Gosh, you must be tired running around all day. Can't even offer you a glass of water, can I?'

There was no answer. Priti took a blue bottle out of her sling bag and sipped from the nozzle. On a whim, Meera stepped aside and opened the door wide. From where she stood, Priti could see the chair where Roshan sat.

'Roshan, say hello to our benefactor. Priti lives down at Kamani house.'

'Oh, is that right? Well, you are being very neighbourly.' Roshan smiled at her.

'It's no problem, sir. I come to many of the buildings in the area. And not just with medicines.'

Meera looked up. 'Really? I thought Helping Hand was only for medical items.'

'It started that way, but very often people we visit ask us to bring over some food stuff and how can we refuse? They need to eat too, right? Also, many of them don't trust the online sites; any way their delivery dates have become so erratic.'

'Be careful now. Before you know it, they will be handing you entire shopping lists.'

Priti laughed. 'No, no, ma'am. And I don't mind, the idea is to help people, right? What difference does it make to me if it's milk or medicines?'

'And what do you do, Priti, if you don't mind me asking?' asked Roshan.

'I am a TV scriptwriter. But I'm not getting new work anymore, so thought I would volunteer for this service. Started with two hours in the morning and afternoon – ten to twelve, five to seven, but now it's pretty much all day.'

'Told you, it will take over your life. You have no idea how many of us there are,' Meera laughed.

'Ha ha. To be honest, I enjoy it, ma'am. Gets me out of the house. I can talk to people, however briefly, and be of actual help. Better than watching those horror stories on TV all day. It gets me down.'

'Well, we are glad you feel that way. Else we may have added to the numbers you see flashing on your screen. The dear departed,' Roshan quipped. He was in good spirits; he seldom spoke so much to strangers, leave alone crack jokes.

'So, where next, on your errands?' Meera asked.

'Oh, your building only. Wing D. You must know them, a Mrs Mehta.'

'What, Ruby Mehta? But...' Roshan blurted out, before Meera gave him a look.

'Why, is something wrong?'

'No, it's nothing. Let us not hold you up then,' Meera said.

Priti put the bottle back into her satchel.

'You will think I am crazy, but can I say something, if you won't mind?' Meera asked.

'Of course, ma'am.'

'I baked a cake yesterday. Would you like to carry a slice of it with you?'

'Meera...'

'It's in the oven. I haven't tasted it yet. And I'll be extra careful.' And as if to demonstrate that she applied some sanitizer from the dispenser on the shoe rack next to the door.

'I can cut a slice and put it in a paper bag for you to carry back. You look like you could do with a snack.'

There was no stopping her. Roshan watched, a look of distress on his face. But to his relief, Priti said, 'I would love that, ma'am. Will have it on my way back. Thank you.'

Meera's face lit up. She rushed off towards the kitchen before the girl could change her mind. Roshan made a gesture with his palms turned upward, though he was grateful that she had accepted the offer.

Meera returned with a small packet and handed it to Priti. She extended the dispenser and Priti took some.

'It's an orange blossom cake, hope you like it.'

'Wow, I am sure I will. Thank you so much, ma'am. And please call if you need anything else, okay? Bye sir, stay safe.' She waved to Roshan and was on her way.

Meera turned to face Roshan with a triumphant look on her face.

'Well?'

'Well, what?'

'You were about to object, I thought.'

'No, I'm glad she took it. But the volunteers must have rules, dos and don'ts, you know. I felt you may have put her in a spot.'

'People aren't getting it from food. And I disinfected the package in front of you.'

'Yes. I am not complaining, Meera. It was nice to talk to someone after so long. Other than you, that is.'

'Yes, wasn't it? You want some?'

'What? Oh, sure, why not? Before it's all given away to people at the door...'

As they sat eating cake, Priti rang the bell at the Mehta residence. She had left their bag of groceries and vegetables with the D-wing guard, to avoid lugging it around. A plump lady in a purple dressing gown opened the door. Priti placed her in her late sixties.

'Oh, from Helping Hand, are you? So punctual. What's happened to those big guys, huh? There for all those big Diwali sales, but gone when we need them. Now they are saying, deliveries will start only by end of month. You tell me, who will wait for 20 days for breakfast cereal? You got everything I mentioned in the list?'

'Yes, ma'am. More or less. There was no *methi saag*. The rest is all there. Here are the bills.'

Mrs Mehta read the list.

'Bell peppers are 300 a kilo, is it? Well, these vendors will make a killing now, but what can be done about it? Please wait, I'll come back with the money.'

She walked away with the bag. From the landing, Priti looked out on to the road. There was not a soul in sight. Only a dog lay listlessly in the sun. When she turned around, there was a little girl standing at the door. Priti was startled.

'Oh hi, what's your name?'

'Divya. Who are you?'

'I am Priti. I came with some things for... your grandma? You live in this house?'

The girl nodded.

'Where are your parents?'

She turned and pointed to the inside of the house. 'Watching TV.'

'Divya, what are you doing here? Go inside, now!'

Mrs Mehta handed Priti the money, rolling her eyes. Then she quickly became sheepish. Priti took the money and walked down the stairs without another word. Mrs Mehta called out a thank you behind her.

Walking out of the building gate, Priti saw a young woman sitting on the pavement with two tiny children. Priti had seen her begging before. The children stared at Priti, expectantly.

She looked in her bag to check if she had any candy but couldn't find any. Then something rustled – it was the paper bag with Meera's cake. She thought for a moment, then took it out. It was a generous helping. The fragrance filled her nostrils, and she felt hungry. She broke the piece into two and gave the bag to the mother. The older child snatched it from her hand. Priti walked away. The D-wing drop had been her last errand for the day. Usually, she felt a lift on her way back home in the evening, but today she carried only a stab of irritation.

~

The week passed by slowly. There were rumours of the lockdown being lifted, which, for some unfathomable reason, filled Meera with hope, as if she had plans to dine or shop the moment it was – or even have the maid come over to relieve her of daily chores. She knew all that would have to wait for much longer, at least for them.

'Can you imagine a future where we will look back at this dreadful time and wonder how we came through?' she asked Roshan once.

'Easier to imagine you sitting alone reminiscing about me, our life together,' Roshan replied, with the same morbid streak that stained his wit of late.

'Oh, shut up. What a terrible thing to say, Roshan.'

She tried to fill her days with housework, so that the time would pass. As the days passed, Roshan became even more withdrawn and she missed a real conversation. There wasn't anyone to call, and she didn't want to bother Maya too often; she had her own troubles to deal with. Though Maya herself had called, twice in the past month, to talk about matters she couldn't bring up during their Zoom chats – to know if Meera wanted her to come back home. The first time Maya brought it up, she wasn't prepared but the next time, Meera said she did not. It made little sense for Maya to throw away a career, built over years. A live-in help – Meera would see about that, when the time came. And they had left it at that.

The fridge appeared emptier every day and one Friday, Meera began to look up the online sites. The organic store she had ordered from in the past said they were not taking orders. Another couldn't promise a fixed delivery date. There was one store which seemed to be operating, but Meera didn't place an order. She mentioned the first two to Roshan and asked what she should do.

'Why, what happened to your friend from Kamani house? Didn't she say she would deliver anything?'

'Are you being sarcastic?'

'No. Call her and see. The delivery boys from the stores will only dump the stuff at the gate and be off. Either you will have to go down or beg the guard to lug it up. The girl may be better that way, don't you think?'

That was all the prodding Meera needed. She whipped her phone out and called Priti.

'Hi, Priti? This is Meera from Silver Crest Apartments, you came by the other day…'

'Of course, ma'am. How are you?'

'We are well, thank you. Hope you are well too?'

'I am fine. What can I get you this time, ma'am?'

'So you are still volunteering with Helping Hand? I feel shameless asking you, but we do need a few things and the sites are still not reliable.'

'Of course. I am doing my runs. Could you WhatsApp me your list please? I have already taken all the orders I can handle today, but I can get it done tomorrow morning for sure, if that's not a problem.'

'That's totally fine, Priti. But this time, it's not medicines. Could I request you to pick up some groceries, if you don't mind?'

'Ma'am, please don't be so hesitant. It's all available under one roof at the *bhandar*.

Just send me your list. No worries at all. And is sir doing alright?

'Yes, he is. I'll send you the list right away. Thank you so much, you are a godsend.'

Roshan looked at her flushed face and shrugged as if to say, 'Look how easy that was.'

Meera started on her list, keeping the most essential items in, knocking off superfluous ones.

'Do you remember whether they stock canned tuna at the *bhandar*, Roshan?'

'Tuna? Isn't it called the *Shakahari Bhandar*? Or is it *sahakari*?'

'Very funny.'

'I only care about my Royce chocolates, and that's not to be found now, for love or money.'

Meera sent her list to Priti and received a prompt reply. Priti would deliver the rations at ten in the morning. She went into the kitchen and checked – half of the cake was still there; she decided to bake some biscottis anyway. Roshan liked them too.

After breakfast the next morning, Meera had a bath, wore her favourite white tunic and waited for the bell to ring. She wondered if Roshan would take the trouble to shave but he emerged from the bathroom in his pyjamas, unshaven, with unkempt hair, sleep in his eyes.

It was a jaunty ring today, two quick toots. Cheery, not impatient.

'Hi, ma'am. Good to see you again. All well?'

'Yes. God, did I make you carry so many things up?' The bag on the floor at Priti's feet did look heavy.

'You know what, ma'am? A truck with fresh veggies had just come in, so I took the liberty of getting a few extra things. You can always use them at a time like this, right?'

'How wonderful. That's so thoughtful of you, Priti. Let me take the bag in.'

Priti made as if to pick it up, then stepped away awkwardly, letting Meera fetch it.

When Meera went in, Priti put her head round the door and called out, 'Good morning, sir! How are you today?'

'I'm good. Courtesy the good folks at the Helping Hand, we are well looked after, thank you very much.'

Priti laughed loudly.

'What's so funny?' Meera asked.

'Sir is. He must be making you laugh all the time, no?'

'Well, he does sometimes, when he is in the mood. But it's only the two of us, and we also get tired of seeing just each other's faces.'

'I know what you mean.' Meera could sense that behind her mask, Priti had made a sympathetic face.

'Long day ahead?'

'Yeah. More people have come to know about us, so the calls are piling up. Also, some of the volunteers have dropped out.'

'Why, has anyone…'

'No, no. We haven't had a single case yet. To be doubly sure, we are all tested every weekend. Can't be too careful, right?'

'Yes. But once this lockdown is over, you will have to get back to work again. Will it be from home you think, for a while?'

'Oh, for sure. Even meetings with the channels will be on Zoom or Skype. Can't say I am happy about it. I'll go mad, staying in the house all day. So many questions every time you step out, you know?'

'Good time to get married, I say,' Roshan quipped.

Priti laughed at that. 'That reminds me. You heard, ma'am, someone had a child in a village in UP, and called her Corona? Can you believe it?'

'Oh, totally. Why, Meera and I had gone to Shillong, back in the day, and the two girls at the hotel reception were the good sisters Goodness and Unity. I am serious. So, for all you know, the twins Quarantino and Lockdown Lyngdoh have made their arrival in some charming household there,' said Roshan with a straight face.

It was Meera's turn to laugh now. Later she would think how odd it was, this banter in the doorway between the three of them. Then she remembered the cake.

'Priti, I have baked some biscottis. Let me give you some for the day?'

'Now you are spoiling me, ma'am. The cake was amazing, by the way. Better than the posh bakeries. Really.'

'Oh, thank you. You know there's quite a bit of it left, let me throw in another slice with your biscotti, alright?'

'Yay, thank you.'

'When all this is over, you must come and have a meal with us. Meera is an exceptional cook, you know,' Roshan said.

'I would love to. Thank you, sir.'

'Here you go,' Meera said, handing her the packet.

'Thank you. Till next time then, ma'am. Call as soon as the stuff runs out and just give me a day's notice, okay? And please, you don't have to bake a cake every time you ask for me!'

'Well, it's something to look forward to, isn't it now? A welcome visitor, in these times. Bye, have a nice day.'

On the way down, Priti opened the packet and broke off a piece of the cake. Surprised at how good it was, she wolfed it down before she had even reached the building gate. The beggar children came running as soon as she emerged. This time she did have some toffees in the bag, and she handed them out. They looked disappointed.

The next morning, Meera decided to go downstairs for a stroll in the compound. It had been over ten days since she left the house.

'Do you need to? You are already quite active around the house, unlike me,' said Roshan.

'Yes, but stepping outside is different. A bit of sun on your skin, some fresh air. Don't worry, I'll stay away from the guards. Just a few rounds around the compound and back home.'

As she was putting on her walking shoes, Roshan noticed a small bundle next to her.

'What's that?'

'It's for Malti.'

'Malti?'

'Ah, the beggar girl outside our gate. You've seen her. The one who moves around on a wooden skateboard with wheels, remember?'

'Yes. And what are you giving her?'

'The rest of the cake. I am tired of eating it. Will be a treat for her kids.'

'I see. Quite the local Mary Antoinette...'

'Hush!'

Meera walked out, leaving the house door ajar; Roshan could hear her giggling outside.

The guard came running at the sight of her.

'Has anything happened, ma'am?'

'Nothing at all. Just came down to stretch my legs. Keep sitting.'

The compound was deserted. Only the stray cats, adopted by the security guards, peered out from behind potted plants. At the main gate, she asked the head guard, 'Someone's still feeding the cats, I hope?'

'Yes, ma'am. Every day. They are happy.'

The gate was shut but through the grille, Meera saw Malti combing the hair of one of her girls. She called out for her. Malti dropped the comb on the pavement and rolled her board towards the gate.

'Don't come too close now. Here, Shyam, give these to her, will you?'

Meera gave the guard some money and the paper bag. He opened the door and handed it over. Malti folded her hands in thanks and tucked the money into her blouse.

Then she opened the packet and took the cake out. She seemed perplexed. Strangely, she lifted it to her nose, and exclaimed, 'Oh, it came from your house, this thing!'

'What do you mean?'

'*Arrey*, the other day, a young girl walked out from the building and gave us a piece of this. The children ate most of it, I had a small corner. It was very nice.'

Meera walked back quietly towards their block. Somehow, she didn't feel like doing the rounds any longer.

When she entered the flat, Roshan said, 'Back already? That was a very short walk!'

'I didn't say I was going out for an hour, did I,' she said testily, before adding in a gentler tone, 'The sun is too strong, didn't feel like it.'

Meera walked into the bedroom, then sat on the bed for a few moments before dragging herself back to the hall. Roshan was reading something on his phone and she tiptoed away.

Predictably, the lockdown got extended again. There were too many cases, and as Roshan put it, it was like riding a tiger – once on it, it was not easy to get off. Provisions in the kitchen began to dwindle again and one day, there was a call from Priti, asking if they needed supplies.

'Thanks, Priti, but we won't need to trouble you anymore. Online deliveries have picked up again. Thanks for asking though. Take care.'

Roshan heard this exchange, surprised. 'Really? I didn't know that.'

'What? Yes, they are taking orders, I must have forgotten to mention it. And I spoke to Shyam at the gate, he will bring it up. No point troubling the girl repeatedly.'

'Okay. But I thought you sounded a bit curt, that's all.'

Meera didn't answer. She stared at the little yellow sunbird that had alighted on their windowsill. It looked this way and that, let out a few squeaks and flew away.

~

6

Shelter from the Storm

I couldn't believe we had survived the night. When the tall windows of the prayer room, where the idols were kept, fell in last night, I had prepared myself for the end. Didi Moni was locked in her room with her father, as secure as she could possibly be in the middle of such havoc, and I had run to Raja Babu's bedside, to see that he was comfortable till the end. That was my place, to be dutifully present by the man who was everything to me – guardian, provider, guide – since the day I came to live in this palace, as a toddler. He was ninety, which made me no less than seventy, and we would face our fate as old men together.

Yet, to my surprise, it was Raja Babu's feeble voice that woke me, as I sat slouched in slumber, propped against the carved wooden leg of his majestic four poster.

'Haradhon, get up. It's morning. The storm has passed.'

For a moment, I thought I was dreaming. How could such a storm have passed without destroying everything in its path? In my entire life, I hadn't seen anything like it, never knew the elements were capable of such fury.

I stood up and touched his feet.

'Shall I get your tea, Raja Babu?'

'That can wait. Go see if everyone is alright first. Come and tell me that Ruku is fine.'

I ran off. It was the first thing that had occurred to me too, to check if Didi Moni was safe. She was the heart of this ancient *rajbari*, its infant queen. All of us – her grandfather, father, me – doted on her such that it was impossible to even contemplate any harm could befall her.

I was sure I would find her sleeping peacefully in her father's arms, but the sight which confronted me the moment I set foot outside Raja Babu's room brought my fears rushing back. From the verandah, I saw our age-old mango tree spread-eagled on the courtyard; the stone platform around its base shattered to a hundred pieces, roots thick as limbs jutting out into the air. In its fall, the grand old tree had claimed the marble head of the man who built this palace many hundred years ago – Raja Radhacharan Basak. The statue now lay severed from the bust, nestling between the branches of the fallen tree. The lord's name appeared unbidden to my lips at this most unholy of omens. These deaths were not of mere objects, but very much of the family I had grown up with. The magnificent tree, under which I had spent many a summer afternoon, contemplating the ebb and flow of the fortunes of this distinguished household; the marble bust which reassured me that royalty never died – it rose, eventually, above any challenge, to regain its former glory. Yet now these things lay in the dust, humbled by an angry breath from Mother Nature. How puny they seemed. I turned my face away as if my gaze would only embarrass them further.

I feel I should tell you a bit about this palace and its inhabitants, before going any further. After all, there are no rajas left in Bengal, nor *rajbaris* in the strict sense of the word. But mere laws, or nomenclatures, can never change a man's station in this world. A king is always a king – blue blood runs in his veins, however diminished his circumstances may be. If there is one thing I have learnt over the years, it is this.

Raja Babu's great – many times over great – grandfather was Raja Radhacharan Basak, who in his day was reputed to be the richest man in this land. He was a friend of the British and made his fortune selling textiles to them. Raja Babu says he owned 35 houses in the Shovabajar area and even the Shovabajar Rajbari – which stands to this day – belonged originally to him. Everywhere I walk, stretching from Kumartuli to Bagbajar, I see signs of this great family – the Jagannath Ghat by the Hooghly, the Kali Temple, the old thread factory – all built by the Basaks, and my chest swells with pride as if I were one of them. It is true that their noble blood doesn't run in me, but I consider myself a part of this family. I was taken in by a young Raja Babu, after my own father – Raja Babu's father's loyal servant – died from a sudden illness. I was not even a year old then and have no recollection of his face. There isn't even an old picture – who takes a servant's picture? – to remember him by. The only faces I recall are of Raja Babu, and Rani Ma, who ensured I didn't suffer the fate of a street urchin.

But let me return to the Basaks; after all, this is their story. After Raja Radhacharan's demise, the fortunes of the Basak family began to wane. But a giant tree takes a long time to die, and the decline was gradual, albeit steady, such that by the time India became independent of British rule, very little was left of the old glory. The palace remained, along with a few other stately buildings in the neighbourhood, but there wasn't enough money for even their upkeep. Growing up, I saw how tough things were out here, often wondering how a raja could be reduced to such circumstances. What never diminished though, was the goodwill the household enjoyed in this area. The sweet shop owners would come with clay pots of *rosogolla* for the family, never asking for payment, as did the fishmonger and florist. As a young man, when I asked the confectioner how he could keep offering these gifts, he had wiped tears from his eyes and said, 'I have heard stories from my father about the generosity of this *rajbari*. We have all grown in its shade. Everyone goes through good times and bad, does that mean a raja won't have sweets after his meal?'

It gives me great satisfaction to see that things are on the mend again, following the downturn that lasted a few generations. Raja Babu's son, Amiya – Dada Babu to me – is a chip off the same old block his great ancestor was made of. With dogged determination, he managed to evict the tenants and squatters from three of the old Basak buildings and got contractors to build apartment blocks there. So began the recovery in the family's fortunes. Two of the other palatial houses by the river have since been converted into boutique hotels, yielding a steady income through the year. Old debts have been cleared off and Raja Babu no longer has to face the ignominy of being hounded by claimants.

One by one, the wings of the *rajbari*, which had fallen into disrepair, have been restored, and now the palace shines as it must have in its heyday, so much so that even crowds – led by local guides – flock to admire it on weekends. Some say it looks even grander than the Shovabajar Rajbari, at which you can imagine my delight. But Dada Babu's greatest gift to this palace was that of Didi Moni.

For many years, Dada Babu's hands had been too full, with the job of pulling this family back from the brink of ruin, to find the time to marry and produce an heir.

Raja Babu fretted about it, confiding in me sometimes, 'Haradhon, what will become of this palace after Amiya? What good is the resurrection of the Basak name, if there is no one to carry it forward, you say?'

And then one day, six years ago, shortly after the passing of Rani Ma, Dada Babu came home with a newborn child in his arms. At first, heated words were exchanged between Raja Babu and his son. I couldn't make out what the row was about. Yet, who could remain angry after seeing that angelic face? The story of Didi Moni's mother remains a mystery to this day – it isn't my place to broach the subject with either of them. But only a blind man can doubt that Dada Babu is her father. She is a little Basak to the core, the spitting image of her father, just a shade darker.

And it was to her room that I now proceeded, having steadied myself from the shock of the carnage on display in our courtyard. I didn't have to knock, as I heard her lilting voice from within the room.

'Baba, why is the fan off? Aren't you feeling hot? See, my neck is damp with sweat.'

I realized that the power supply had been cut off; the falling trees must have brought down the overhead lines. But everyone was safe, that is what mattered most.

I knocked on the door and asked, 'Dada Babu, shall I get your tea?'

The door opened.

'Haradhon, are you alright? Baba…'

'Raja Babu is fine. I was by his bedside all night. What a night!'

'Don't remind me. Let me go and see Baba, then you and I can take a round and inspect the damage.'

I told him about the tree and the statue, but he seemed unaffected. Unlike his father, Dada Babu was not sentimental. Maybe it was those hard years that made him so.

While Dada Babu was in Raja Babu's room, I checked on the rest of the staff. Ratan, the driver, hadn't arrived yet, but thankfully the car was safely locked away in the garage. The full-time servants – cook Minoti, cleaner Charu and shopper-cum-errand boy Montu – were all in one piece, shaken but unhurt. Minoti's primary concern was whether the late Rani Ma's idols of Balgopal and Vishnu-Lakshmi were intact; no prospect more inauspicious in her eyes than if they had shattered. I didn't mention that the windows of the prayer room had caved in. Montu asked if he should gather the raw mangoes littered all over the courtyard.

The damage to the house was considerable. Windows had shattered, entire doors ripped off their hinges, the roof of the pumphouse gone, ornate glass lamps on either side of the gate smashed. Water had seeped into some rooms on the ground floor, soaking the old carpets. I was sure there was much more. And all this to a sturdy, age old structure built of the best material; I shuddered to think what may have happened to the flimsy shanties and hutments of the poor. Meanwhile, a weak sun had emerged through the clouds and in its light, Dada Babu and I stepped out of the palace gate. There were trees littered everywhere, lamp posts bent like twigs by the gale; but what took us by surprise was the sheer number of people squatting on the road outside, who rose to their feet as soon as we emerged from the gate. None of the faces were familiar to me. I didn't count, but there must have been at least a few hundred of them, all standing with hands folded, staring at Dada Babu. We looked at each other – who were these people?

Perhaps one disaster dwarfs another, for I forgot all about the raging pandemic for a moment and approached one of them, asking where they came from.

'Rajasthan. We are labourers, returning to our homes. Reached Kolkata day before on a Shramik train. Our onward travel arrangements weren't ready because of the weather alert, so we took refuge around the ghats here, but last night we fled from there. We have nowhere to go.'

'And where is home for you?'

He mentioned the names of nearby villages – Kaliachak, Lalgola, Bolpur, Kalyani, Sarsuna, Dhaniakhali. I was amazed at how far they had travelled from their homes, in search of a living, some even with families.

'But why have you gathered here? Shouldn't you go to the nearest police station or somewhere where they can help you?'

'Some of us did, but who has time to listen today? Everything has gone haywire, they are all running helter-skelter; there is so much damage everywhere in the city. We have nothing to eat. Someone said, go to the *rajbari*, maybe they will give you shelter.'

I turned and walked back to Dada Babu, who had wisely kept a distance. It struck me then that neither of us had covered our faces, and these were migrant workers who had arrived from a state badly affected by the disease. As I narrated what the man had said to me, I saw, to my alarm, Didi Moni standing at the gate, holding on to one of the metal railings and gazing intently at the crowd.

Dada Babu heard me out and said, 'I don't know how many of them are here, must be hundreds. Convey my sympathies and tell them that at best, I can give them 3,000-4,000 rupees to buy some food. But beyond that, it's impossible for me to help. We are a small household, they will have to go to the state administration…'

Before he could finish, two women from the group walked up to us, with children – at least a dozen of them – in tow. I motioned to them to stop their advance and keep some distance between us.

'Babu, at least take these children in for some time. Where will we drag them along, begging for help? They are hungry. If the storm lets up, we will leave on our own.'

Two of the girls were crying. The others gaped at Didi Moni. Dada Babu had not noticed her arrival and nearly jumped when she asked, from right behind him, 'What happened to these people?'

'Ruku! What are you doing here? You cannot come out like this. Go inside, right now. Haradhon, take her in…'

Didi Moni ignored us completely. She looked up at the woman who had spoken and asked, 'Why are they crying?'

'They haven't eaten anything since yesterday morning, *ma*. They are hungry.'

Didi Moni's eyes began to water. She turned and ran back into the house. Dada Babu followed.

I was at my wits' end, with no idea what to do with this crowd of help seekers. I made a non-committal gesture, hoping to convey that I was going back in to see if some help could be arranged, and walked away, firmly latching the gate behind me. The men didn't look menacing to me, but I had seen how easily distress and desperation could make men do things they wouldn't ordinarily do.

From the staircase, I could hear Didi Moni's wails and the voices of the men trying to pacify her. On reaching the verandah, I saw Raja Babu trying to pick her up from the floor, as Dada Babu looked on in exasperation. This was another thing – whenever Didi Moni was sad, or angry, she would lie down on the floor, wherever she may be – indoors or outdoors – and cry her heart out. It was difficult to console her. Having not witnessed the scene outside, Raja Babu was naturally confounded and looked towards me enquiringly. I gave him a brief, remembering to mention that Dada Babu had offered them money to buy food.

'Got it. But why is my Ruku upset?'

I looked towards Dada Babu, not wishing to speak out of turn.

'There were some children there, Baba,' Dada Babu informed his father. 'The women said they hadn't eaten since yesterday, that may have...'

Raja Babu looked affectionately towards the girl, whose wails had now reduced to whimpers.

'Oho. Ruku, you felt sad at their plight? But it's only natural, who would not? Come, let us go and see what can be done about it.'

Ruku got up immediately from the floor.

'Baba! They are migrants who arrived on a train from Rajasthan yesterday. Many may even be ill. You shouldn't go anywhere near them, nor Ruku.'

It was hard to disagree with Dada Babu; we had been careless ourselves.

But Ruku said, 'We will wear masks and gloves. *Jethu*, where are the masks?'

Raja Babu knew there was no backing out now, so he said, 'Okay, but we will go only till our gate, not close to them, Ruku. We will be on this side, they on the other, agreed?'

Ruku nodded vigorously. I went into the room to fetch the masks. Dada Babu could barely hide his frustration, but with his father and daughter on one side, he was in a bind. Once I had given everyone their mask and tied a cloth around my own mouth, we trooped down again.

By now, the staff had gathered too, and I heard Minoti and Charu berating Montu, 'Where will they go, you think? Hotels in Chowringhee, ha? Just because you have a roof over your head...'

On seeing us, they fell quiet and stood aside. Raja Babu walked up to the marble head, now placed on the floor of the verandah. He shook his head.

'Omi, do you think it can be joined to the bust again?'

'I doubt it, Baba. But we can try and install the head on a new base. I'll see what can be done.'

Didi Moni was getting restless again. She caught hold of Raja Babu's hand and pulled him towards the gate. The crowd was still there, but I was relieved to see they hadn't advanced further. Raja Babu peered through the grille of the gate and beckoned to them. I ran up to his side and shouted, 'Don't come too close. Stand a bit away and answer Raja Babu's questions.'

If Raja Babu was displeased at my intervention, he didn't show it.

Only two people stepped forward, a man and a woman. They had now covered their faces, which was a relief. I could see hope in their eyes; perhaps they felt that this unlikely pair – a very old man and a little girl – were more likely to show kindness.

'So, how many of you are here? I can't make out,' Raja Babu asked.

The man appeared unsure.

'Maybe a hundred, *babu*, maybe more.'

'Oh. And how many women and children?'

This was easier to figure out; the woman turned around and did a quick count.

'*Babu*, around 15 of us, and 10-12 children.'

Raja Babu looked down at Didi Moni.

'Ruku, what should we do, you think – feed the children and women first, then the men?'

Ruku nodded, her tears gone. Her eyes shone with purpose.

Dada Babu watched this exchange, his mouth open, looking like he couldn't believe his ears. Minoti and Charu walked up closer, as if to convey they were part of this plan, whatever shape it took.

'Dadu, let's take the children in. They can stay in one of the rooms downstairs, no?' said Ruku, pointing towards the row of rooms along the verandah.

'Right, that's a good idea. Haradhon, which room shall we open? How about the smaller *sabhaghar*, it won't have much by way of furniture. Maybe we roll carpets out on the floor and they can rest there?'

'Baba...' Dada Babu tried to intervene, but Raja Babu simply lifted a palm and stopped him. I had a vision of the old Raja Babu, in his prime, sans dominion, but with a king's blood still boiling in him. His authority stirred something in me. Even the staff stared at him in awe.

'Minoti, will you feel scared to cook for them?'

'Not a bit, Raja Babu. You just tell us what to do. We have our faces covered, they have theirs. What is there to fear?'

'Good. Tell me, what is easiest to rustle up quickly?'

It was Ruku who answered. 'Bread, eggs and milk.'

'Shabash! Where is Montu? Come here. Take money from Dada Babu and go to all the shops in the market. Buy as many eggs and loaves you can lay your hands on, and packets of milk. Has Ratan arrived? When he comes, both of you go back together and get a sack of rice and a few kilos of dal. Ask Minoti what else she needs.'

Montu stood there, gaping at him, as if he had been given directions to plunge into the river.

'What happened? Didn't you hear Raja Babu? Fetch the bags and get going,' I said, a bit harshly.

Raja Babu turned to Charu. 'Charu, prepare the *sabhaghar*. When you are ready, Haradhon will ensure that only the women and children go in there, and then he can close the door behind them. It will not do for them to be walking all over this house. Keep an eye on Ruku. And Minoti, the moment Montu is back, boil the eggs, give them all four pieces of bread and two eggs each and some tea. Give the children a glass of milk. This shouldn't be difficult. And then, wait for my instructions.'

He turned to the couple outside the gate.

'We will try to help. But please appreciate that there are only a few of us, and we will need you to be patient. First, we feed the children and women, but soon, all of you. Wait outside, Haradhon here will guide you.'

'Thank you, *babu*,' they said, with folded hands.

'Not me, thank this little girl.'

Raja Babu motioned to Dada Babu to join him upstairs, and walked away, hand in hand with Didi Moni. I usually keep some money for household expenditure with me, and I gave this to Montu. He ran off to do the errands. Minoti and Charu went in search of the keys to the *sabhaghar*.

I hadn't been called upstairs but, unable to contain my curiosity, tiptoed up the stairs and stood just below the first-floor landing, where they couldn't see me from the verandah.

Raja Babu was saying, 'Omi, I know you won't be happy, but Ruku is right. How can we not help these people? Just look at their state. God knows how many hours they have travelled on a train and then to land up in the middle of this deluge. We have a duty to them, don't we?'

'But Baba, so many? A few of them, I could still have understood. There may be 200 people outside!'

I couldn't see Raja Babu from where I was, but knew that a smile had appeared on his face from the tone of his voice.

'Omi, Omi, 200 is not that unusual a number to knock on the gates of a *rajbari* when in need. You haven't seen, but I have. That is a lesson I learnt at my father's knees – with wealth comes responsibility. Without it, you only retain your wealth, but lose all respect.'

Dada Babu's voice sounded choked, as if he was stung by this rebuke. 'I never said anything about not helping them…'

'I know, Omi. You are my son, after all. And you have done much more for this household than I ever could. But that is even more reason for you to help wholeheartedly today. The name that you are trying to resurrect, won't be achieved simply by restoring this palace and growing our fortune, but by showing the world the largeness of our hearts. Without a heart, a king is only a despot.'

To another, this may have sounded like the sentimental babble of a senile, old man, but it moved me to my core and I wept freely.

'Note Ruku's first instinct – it was to help the hungry girl. I have never felt prouder of anyone in the family. That is the spirit of this house. Why, look at Minoti. She is a simple woman, but see the eagerness with which she offered to help, with such little regard for her personal safety. They have all imbibed this from your mother, Omi. Do you remember the lines of people who came by when she passed away? Why, is it for our status, you think? Wrong. Every other merchant in Bagbajar is wealthier than us today, but it's not the same thing.'

There was a pause. Then Didi Moni's voice floated up.

'Dadu, what will the men eat?'

'Yes, that's a good question, Ruku. You have any suggestions?'

'*Khichudi*!' she said, and clapped her hands.

I heard Dada Babu's laughter and felt relieved. Without his participation, this venture was doomed. Guessing that the moment was now right, I cleared my throat, to alert them of my presence, and emerged on the landing.

'Ah Haradhon, did Montu return with the foodstuff?'

'He should be back soon, but I wanted to ask about our plans. Once the women and children have moved into the meeting room, what should I tell the men waiting outside? Will they spend the night here as well?'

It was Dada Babu who answered this time.

'We cannot keep the women inside and have the men sleep on pavements. Who knows, we may get more rain today. Baba, I was thinking…'

'Yes?'

'I know they are many in number, but what if we open up the puja hall? That is the largest space in this house and can easily accommodate many of them. We have those large tarpaulin sheets stored somewhere. Maybe we can roll them out and they can all shack up. What do you say?'

A smile lit up Raja Babu's sunken face.

'Excellent, Omi! I couldn't have thought of a better solution myself. You know, I was thinking of that hall just the other day; it's been six years since we had a puja there. Since Nirmala… Why, poor Ruku hasn't seen a proper Durga Puja in this house! Let's open it up, Omi.

There's no greater homage to the goddess than the service of our own brethren.'

Dada Babu stormed into his bedroom and emerged with a large metal ring with keys on it.

'Come, Haradhon Da, let's open the doors and see what state it is in,' he called out to me, marching down the corridor, a new energy in his stride. I could feel that another raja had woken from his slumber.

'I am also coming,' yelped Ruku in delight, and together we skipped down the stairs.

In the courtyard, we ran into Montu. On being asked if he had managed to procure the rations, he exclaimed, 'You won't believe the state the market is in. Half the roofs gone, the tin walls all twisted out of shape, ankle-deep water everywhere…'

He had a habit of exaggeration, so I stopped him right there.

'Did you find the things or not?'

'Yes, I managed to, some from one shop, some from another. Whatever was left in stock, but I will have to go back for the rice. Ratan Da is here.'

Ruku, who had been listening, asked, 'Are all the eggs broken then?'

Minoti had water set to boil and she went about her job immediately. Before Dada Babu could proceed to the puja hall, I suggested we get the women and children settled in the meeting room, as their meal would be ready soon. Dada Babu agreed and asked me to open the gate.

'Ruku, wear your mask, and stand here with me. No running to them the moment they enter, okay?'

Ruku nodded demurely, suddenly obedient.

I opened the gate and asked the women and children to stand in a file. I felt like a general – lieutenant at least – overseeing a hazardous mission.

'All of you are aware that a distance needs to be maintained, so start moving in a line towards the room prepared for you. It has a toilet, which you can use, in turns, to wash up. Unfortunately, the electricity has gone after the storm, so the fans won't work. I will have some food sent once you have settled in.'

They walked in, staring at the house in open wonderment – it must have been unlike anything they had seen before. The door to the *sabhaghar* was open. They walked in quietly and sat down on the floor. Almost on cue, Charu emerged from the kitchen, carrying a large iron kettle in one hand and a tall pile of paper cups in another. She placed the cups in a line on the floor outside the door of the meeting room and tipped steaming milk from the kettle into each of them.

'Can I call them?' Didi Moni asked, but Dada Babu shook his head, holding her firmly by his side.

Charu asked one of the women to come out and carry the glasses inside.

We walked to the puja hall. The big iron lock on the door had rusted, and I had to give it a good tug after turning the key. The door creaked open and we saw the magnificent room for the first time in years. There was a time when this was the very heart of the *rajbari*, and I only had to close my eyes to hear the rhythmic beats of the drum, the conchshells and ululation, the recital of mantras from the stage. Even the whiff of dust that wafted out seemed to hold for me the fragrance of *dhuno* – our frankincense. Didi Moni's voice brought me back to the moment.

'Baba, what a big room; we used to have Durga Puja here? Why don't we have it any more?'

Dada Babu looked at me and sighed. But I remained silent. Some things are better coming from one's own father.

Finally, Dada Babu said, 'Yes, Ruku, we used to have very grand pujas here once upon a time. Haradhon Jethu probably remembers it better than I do. But pujas need a lot of money to organize and we were not in a position to carry on with them. Still, they continued in a small way, till my mother – your *dida* – passed away. After that, we decided to stop.'

'Are we going to start again?'

'Would you want us to?'

'Yes!'

'Fine, let me discuss it with Baba. But today, we have a different purpose for this hall.'

Frankly, I had expected the room to be in worse shape, but other than the dust and minor discolouration of the wall in some places, it seemed fine. Once Montu and I opened the windows out and aired the space, it would be perfectly habitable, assuming the weather held out. I don't know if it was because we were seeing it totally empty, but the hall seemed even larger than I remembered it.

Dada Babu surprised me by saying, 'Go and ask one of the men to come in and see this. But first, take Ruku upstairs.'

Didi Moni was about to protest, but Dada Babu insisted.

I told her, 'Didi Moni, you cannot come close to them. We have to keep you and Raja Babu away from them, right? You can watch everything from the verandah, okay?'

At that, she agreed to come away. I could imagine how utterly riveting all of this was for a child her age.

Raja Babu sat in his armchair on the balcony. I placed Didi Moni's stool next to him. He looked somewhat downcast – maybe it was because of the broken statue.

'How did you find the hall, Haradhon?'

'It's totally fine, Raja Babu. I'm sure they will fit in.'

'Do you remember what grand times we had in that room? The musical events, poetry sessions, plays? Ah, those were the days.'

'There were singers there, Dadu?' Didi Moni asked, her eyes wide.

'Yes, Ruku. You see, your Dadu always thought that if he just shook the mango tree outside, gold would fall from it. He spent like he was the wealthiest man around. Except, he wasn't. So, one day, everything had to stop.'

Raja Babu's sigh pierced through me. I couldn't bear to stand and watch. I mumbled something about the errands and slipped away. All these windows to past memories were bound to open up today as we prepared to lay open the palace for refuge.

As instructed, I led the man – the one who had spoken to us in the morning – to the hall.

He stared at the room and surprised me by asking, 'Who are they?'

He meant the two large canvases that hung on opposite walls of the room. Other than the central chandelier, they were the only adornments the room still possessed; the rest had all been moved to other rooms.

'That,' I said, pointing to the portrait of the man wearing a regal turban and holding a silk shawl in his hand, 'is Raja Radhacharan Basak, the man who built this palace. And that, on the other wall is Raja Madhobcharan Basak, Raja Babu's father. Raja Babu, whom you met this morning.'

'I see. Old family then.'

'Yes, stretching back hundreds of years. And today, you have the good fortune of taking shelter in this ancient palace. All of you will manage, right?'

The man smiled. 'What are you saying, *babu*? We spent the night on the streets. This is more than we could have expected. If we can just have something to eat and rest here till they arrange buses for us…'

'Now that is not for me to decide, let me be clear. You will be fed today and put up for the night. The rest is between you and the owners. Anyway, get three others from outside. You can roll the tarpaulin out.'

I showed him the storeroom where the material was stacked in heavy rolls.

Minoti came by.

'Haradhon Da, Ratan and Montu just dumped sacks of rice and dal at my doorstep, how will I manage to cook for so many people? I have utensils to make for 20 maybe, but not 200!'

'Go upstairs and tell Raja Babu.'

She strode off purposefully. I followed, to ensure that she did not shoot her mouth off. Minoti was a conscientious worker, but could come across as irreverent; often forgetting who she was speaking to.

The moment she presented the problem to them, Dada Babu said, 'I was thinking about that just now, Minoti. Baba, remember the cooks we called during Ma's *shraddho*? So many people turned up that day that you asked Haradhon Da to go and get a team that was equipped to prepare food on a large scale. Who were they, Haradhon Da?'

Dada Babu was right. I kicked myself for not having thought about them earlier.

'The tent house people, Dada Babu. Not fancy caterers but experts at arranging meals for large crowds on short notice – just the kind we need today. Let me call them, though who knows what state they are in today, after last night…'

'Yes, check if they are open at all. The tent house would have been shut for the last two months, you will be lucky to get hold of them,' said Raja Babu.

I called but nobody picked up.

'Let me send Montu to the shop once,' I said.

Montu came back with a hapless looking man, who didn't inspire much confidence in me or Minoti. He said that the shop was not open, but he could get two of his colleagues and come by to do the meals.

'What will you make? And in what?'

'Oh, we will get the cooking pots, don't worry. You just have to give us the fires, and we will manage the rest.'

Dada Babu asked, 'And what can you make quickly? These men are starving.'

'For both times?'

He meant lunch and dinner.

'Guess so. Why, you eat once a day, is it?'

The man smiled sheepishly.

'So, since you have bought some rations, how about *khichudi* and alu *bhaja* now, egg curry rice at night?'

'That's fine. How much will that cost?' Dada Babu asked.

'How about 150 per head, for both meals?'

I butted in. 'We are providing the rice and dal. Make it 100. It's a lot of heads.'

The man bowed his head. I knew the profits would be shared between him and his two friends, the tent house wouldn't see a rupee of it. But how was that our problem? I looked at Dada Babu and he gave me a slight nod.

'Just do a count, Haradhon Da, of both rooms. And keep it quiet, you don't want word to get out, or else there will be a thousand people outside the gate before you know it. Such are the times.'

There were 160 of them in all. Feeding them for just one day would set us back by 20,000 at least, I calculated. With Raja Babu, Dada Babu and Didi Moni safely back upstairs, I went to ask the others to come inside, 10 at a time. Montu, Charu and I stood on the verandah and watched them walk in. I saw Didi Moni looking down from the balcony – head barely clearing the top of the railing – utterly mesmerized by the sight. It was something none of us were ever likely to forget.

The tent house people arrived, carrying huge pots and vessels. Minoti sent Montu to the market again to buy papad and jars of pickle.

'How can they have only *khichudi* and potato fries; this is a *rajbari*,' she said.

I turned away to hide my smile. She had said this in all earnestness.

When the food was ready, one of the tent house men handed out stacks of dried leaf plates. Some of the men sat inside the hall, others squatted around the courtyard in the open, after seeking our permission. I instructed the tent house men to place the vessels in the middle of each setting, and asked the women in the *sabhaghar*, who had had a little something by now, to serve the men. A hundred and sixty people ate, in practically pin-drop silence, not looking up from their plates. I felt something well up inside me and saw that tears flooded Minoti and Charu's faces too.

It was nearly dusk by the time everyone had eaten and the vessels put away. Another round would have to begin soon. Minoti informed me that food had been served upstairs, and I asked them to eat as well. I took some tea on a tray and went upstairs.

Didi Moni was asleep in her room, but Raja Babu and Dada Babu sat discussing the next course of action.

I heard Dada Babu say, 'I called Ghoshal at the police station. He said he would check and let me know. But he warned me that nothing would happen by tomorrow morning as everything was in disarray. Should I call Derek?'

'No, he must be inundated with calls on a day like this. There is so much focus on these inbound workers now, they will organize something soon. Let's give them a day to respond. Anyway, we cannot fix private transport for them. It has to go through the state machinery.'

'And meanwhile…?'

'They stay. What else can we do? We can hardly turn them out tomorrow, having given them shelter for a day. They will stay for a couple of days, till there is a way to get them to their villages. I know this is a strain on you, Omi, but there is really no other way. I am sorry.'

'Don't say that, Baba. It's not the money, just with Ruku running around all over the place…'

'Nothing will happen. We will watch from here, wearing our masks, and before you know it, two days will have passed. And anyway, one day or two, it hardly makes a difference. If it has to happen, it would have happened by now.'

This sounded logical, but I feared it wouldn't exactly play out that way; both Dada Babu and I knew Raja Babu and Didi Moni too well. They were itching to speak to these people. Had it not been for the virus, they would have been sitting right in their midst, exhorting them to recount their experiences.

Sure enough, as the evening grew dark, Raja Babu summoned me and said, 'Haradhon, the man we were speaking to in the morning, can you ask him to come up once?'

I froze. I knew Dada Babu would be dead against it; I myself didn't want to take such a risk. Seeing my hesitation, Raja Babu asked me to call Dada Babu.

'Omi, don't yell, but I wanted to ask one of these men about his journey. I will sit here, at a distance, and he can sit there, near the landing, a good 20 feet away, face covered. Just for a few minutes, okay? Please don't object.'

To my surprise, Dada Babu looked at me and nodded. I went down in search of our man.

In the light of the candles and kerosene lamps – the power supply hadn't been restored yet – the verandah looked like a medieval court scene. At one end, Raja Babu and Dada Babu sat in their chairs, Didi Moni ensconced between them; at the other, a man sat on his haunches with his face half covered, as if about to be sentenced. I stood somewhere halfway between them. The man narrated his story. Most of his group worked as construction labourers, but had lost their jobs when the sites closed down overnight. They had waited for weeks before the trains started plying.

During the narration, his voice sometimes choked with sobs. However, I was struck by the fact that he didn't sound utterly despondent. Rather, it appeared as if he were looking forward to being back in his village and working on the fields again.

Then he asked Raja Babu, '*Babu* was saying this house is hundreds of years old. How does it feel to stay in a house like this, generation after generation?'

The man spoke freely, not tongue-tied by the presence of men of such noble families, as I might have been. His curiosity was frank.

'How can I answer that? Neither I, nor Omi have known anything else. But for every brick in this house, there is a story, that I can tell you. We are such an old family,' Raja Babu answered the man.

Didi Moni, who had been absorbing all this quietly, said, 'Tell us one story, Dadu, please.'

'Yes, *babu*, when will I ever meet people like you again? One story that I can tell my children, when they are older, about the *rajbari* which may have saved our lives.'

Raja Babu laughed and asked Didi Moni, 'What is your full name, Ruku?'

'Rukmini Basak. Why?'

'Good. So, let me tell you about our family name, Basak, and where it came from.'

I was all ears myself – in all these years Raja Babu had never told me this, maybe because I never asked.

'Many hundred years ago, when India was ruled by the great Mughal emperor Akbar, there was a man named Keshob Ram. He was a renowned businessman who imported silk from China to make clothes for the royal family and their courtiers. Akbar liked him very much and gave him the title of *Busakh*. It's a Farsi word meaning a fragrant branch. *Bu* means fragrant, *sakh* is branch of a tree. He thought of Keshob Ram as a fragrant addition to the tree of his empire. That Busakh, over the centuries, has become Basak today.'

Didi Moni clapped and said, 'Rukmini Busakh, what fun! Keshob Ram is part of our family then, Dadu?'

'Yes, indeed. Our line traces back directly to him. What, happy with the story?' Raja Babu asked the man.

'A story befitting this grand house, *babu*. I will tell everyone downstairs right now.'

He stood up and, with some hesitation, asked, '*Babu*, I had a question, if you don't mind. What about tomorrow?'

Dada Babu answered. 'Don't worry. I have spoken to the inspector at the station. By tomorrow, we should have word about your transport. But till that happens, you will be here. Now go down and sleep peacefully.'

The man folded his hands and walked down the stairs.

Amidst the flurry of activity the next day, came news that buses had been arranged to take the workers to their villages. They were to congregate at the Howrah station at 10 the next morning. The news was received with a sigh of relief by all, except Didi Moni. Perhaps she had expected they would stay on for longer. Dada Babu had to explain to her that they too had to reach their own homes, get to work, earn a living again.

In the afternoon, she crept up to me and whispered, '*Jethu*, can you get some chocolates from the market?'

It took me a moment to grasp what she meant – it was for the children in the *sabhaghar*.

'I will, only if you promise that you will not insist on handing them over yourself. You will watch when I give it to them, agreed?'

She smiled and bent her head to one side. I asked her when she wanted me to distribute them. She said just before their departure. It was meant as a parting gift.

The next morning, around eight o'clock, all of us gathered in the verandah downstairs. Many of the men and women milled outside the gate – the courtyard wasn't big enough to hold all. Only a few, led by the man and woman who we had spoken to the first day, stood facing us. The children were also there, chocolate bars in their hands.

'What can we say, *babu*? Except that the experience of the last few weeks had made us so angry, so bitter about people with money and power. But meeting all of you will make us think again. Not everyone in this world is bad. The Mughal king was right in giving your family its name, it fits you. This palace will retain its glory forever, *babu*; and *mamoni*, we will carry your kindness in our hearts till the day we die. Thank you, all. Goodbye.'

Slowly, our guests trudged out the gate, leaving us with leaden feet.

A ray of light had fallen, just at that moment, on the severed marble head of Raja Radhacharan, as if the heavens were blessing the founder of this palace. I knew then that all the storms we were destined to face would pass, and all would be well again.

7
Old Friend

It was while glancing through a news report on his laptop that Abheek suddenly remembered Bunty. These days, there were no newspapers. It was difficult, initially, to do without such an old habit but, as with everything, he had now become used to reading the news on the computer. And since there was no rush to get ready and leave for office, he usually ended up reading more than one, including even a popular Bengali paper online. This particular report had no connection with Bunty, it only spoke about how the official toll in Bengal belied the reality on the ground, as there had hardly been any testing in the state. Suppression was hinted at. Reading about all this stirred up memories from decades ago, and Abheek felt a strange lurch inside. Such capricious things, these memories: coming and going – as they did – at their own bidding, with little consideration for their keepers' comfort. Almost like spirits inhabiting the chambers of our mind, unrestrained by walls of our making, shifting shape, often reclusive, the cause of their sudden appearances unclear. He was thinking about this when Malini came in with his tea.

'Hey, do you remember Bunty, my school friend?'

She had to think for a minute. 'Ah, the guy you bumped into at the Kolkata airport once? I seem to vaguely recollect him – fair, plump fellow, right? Why, what about him?'

'No, nothing. Was reading about Kolkata in the *Anandabazar* and thought of him, for no reason.'

Malini began to hum an old Tagore song that went – *Oh, the good old days of our past, how can we ever forget*, a sarcastic smile on her face. She could be wicked, that way.

But the thought lingered in Abheek's head. Twelve years in the same classroom; there was a time when the two of them were inseparable. People would even say their names together – Bappa-Bunty had gone there, done that. And then one day, Bunty went off to study in the US, and three decades passed with hardly any contact between them.

'Didn't he say he had a restaurant in Cal, or something like that?' Malini asked.

'Yes, yes. I am surprised you remember. Near Deshapriya Park, if I am not mistaken. Must be shut now. What a time it is for these small eateries.'

'Yes. Thank God for salary cheques,' said Malini, somewhat nervously.

Abheek was steadily working his way up the ladder at a global investment bank. He was sure business would be impacted. There were already rumours of furloughs at the New York and Hong Kong offices, but so far nothing in India. Anyway, he wasn't too worried. He had been careful to tuck away the bonuses from good years in prudent investments and they had enough saved. He wondered what kind of financial situation Bunty was in. Growing up, his family was far more comfortable than Abheek's had been. Bunty's father had had a top job at a multinational engineering firm. They lived in a spacious company apartment in a posh housing estate called Tivoli Court and owned a car which was a marker of affluence in those pre-liberalization days. And of course, Bunty went for an undergraduate course to some vague college in Maryland, which they must have put him through. Never a good student, he wasn't the kind to have bagged a full scholarship.

'If you are worried about him, why don't you just call and find out?'

'Call, how? I don't have his number.'

As he said that, Abheek felt a jolt – another spirit surfaced in his head. 4731551. He murmured the number to himself, the landline at Tivoli Court. He still remembered it, how was it possible? In fact, he had to stop himself from calling the number right away. Such a silly notion, as if anyone would answer it. Were Bunty's parents even alive? Anyway, it had been a company flat and Bunty now lived somewhere in south Kolkata, he was sure of it.

'I'll write. Think I have an old mail from him.'

They moved to the table for breakfast. But everything that morning seemed to conspire to drag him back to that time in Kolkata. Malini had made egg parathas, which Chhaya Mashi – Bunty's mother – would often serve for breakfast when Abheek stayed over at their place; the two of them seated on kitchen stools, Mashi doling out the parathas, hot from the skillet, on to their plates.

Abheek's throat felt clogged. He stared at his plate.

'What happened? Not good?'

'Oh, nothing. No, they are great.'

He told Malini about Chhaya Mashi and the parathas.

'Aww. Did you stay over a lot at their place?'

'Practically lived there. It was such a treat for me, you see, after the shabby house I lived in. You've never been to the place I grew up in, you wouldn't know. So, every opportunity I got, I would run to Tivoli Court. They had a big flat. Bunty had no siblings and his parents, mother especially, were really fond of me. My own parents were only too happy to have me out of the house. One mouth less to feed, I guess.'

'God, Abheek, the things you say. It's like you grew up in the gutter!'

'Well, I was just one layer removed from it, actually. Anyway, so yes, I would be there days on end, till Mashi would ask me to go back for some time, out of consideration for my mother I think.'

'How come you have never told me about him? He must have been almost a brother to you.'

'More, maybe. I mean of course, Atreyi was there, but at that age who has much time for his own sister? Also, we were both devils – always up to some mischief or the other.'

Malini laughed. 'That could hardly have endeared you to Bunty's parents.'

'Oh, the real reason for their fondness of me was that I stood first in class, almost always. Now don't ask me how, but I did. And Bengali middle class mothers had – don't know if they still do – this obsession with exam results. If you ranked in school, you could walk on water.'

'And his mum thought some of it would rub off on her son?'

'Guess that was it, though I can confirm that it never worked that way, much to her distress. Bunty remained resolutely away from his books. Actually, the only time I saw some flicker of interest was when he started preparing for his SATs. That was the allure of America, I imagine.'

'Come on, write to him, Abheek. Now you have got me curious. You are obviously still very fond of him.'

Once the plates had been cleared and Abheek had washed up – his contribution to the household chores – he logged on and searched for that old mail from Bunty. Nothing showed up. He was confused. Then, remembering that the mail ID would be under Bunty's proper name, he typed in Shantanu and up it popped. Shantanu Sengupta, that's right. A mail dating back three years, written shortly after their chance encounter at the airport. Bunty had invited Abheek to visit his house when he was in Kolkata next. A sweet enough mail, saying that he was happy to meet Malini and how Abheek hadn't changed much at all, probably meaning his physical appearance. He had signed off with a sentimental – your old friend. Had Abheek even written back? Probably not. He couldn't find a mail trail, at any rate.

He wrote back now, asking how Bunty was coping with the current situation. He even added his mobile number at the bottom, in case Bunty wanted to catch up. This too, he left to him to decide.

The phone rang before an hour had passed. It was an unknown number but Abheek knew it was Bunty, even before he answered.

'Hello?'

'Abheek? Bunty here.'

In his mind's eye, Abheek could almost see the wide goofy grin on his friend's face at the other end of the line. Infectious, it was, that smile – always holding a hint of mischief.

'Bunty! How are you? Such a long time.' Even as he said the words, Abheek was aware that his tone held none of the simple warmth of his friend's voice. Couldn't.

'Surviving, man. But you say. How come you remembered your old friend all of a sudden?'

Not meant as a barb, this; just put forward in Bunty's typical affectionate manner.

'*Arrey*, was reading the *Anandabazar* in the morning and thought of you. Is it true, what they are saying – that there are hundreds of unreported cases in Cal?'

'Hahaha. You grew up here, man. You know the city. Listen then – I went to buy some eggs and stuff at the nearby market yesterday. Man, you should have seen it! Distancing? People were jostling against each other to get to the fish. I am not joking! It was like this virus shit was happening in some other part of the planet. I ran from there! It's scary, I tell you. All these Bongs, they will croak, but with fish fry and *sandesh* in their mouths. Haha.'

Abheek almost choked with laughter. Malini looked on, amused. 'And what's happening with your restaurant. Shut, I guess?'

'Yes, what else? Like every other place. Heaven knows when it will open up now.'

'But you have to keep the staff, right?'

'Of course. Where will they go? They didn't even manage to get back to their villages; so they are all parked in the restaurant, using the kitchen there, sleeping on joined tables. It's my duty to feed them till all this is over. Isn't easy, you know.'

'Oh, and how are folks at home? All good?'

'Folks? You mean my mother? She is fine, spends all her time in front of her gods. I was telling her to throw the other idols out and offer all the sweets to Shani and Shitala, so that we may be spared. Haha.'

There were so many other questions, but Abheek didn't know how to ask them. He said abruptly, 'Well, take care then, Bunty. Give my love to Chhaya Mashi. Let's keep in touch.'

If Bunty was taken aback, it didn't show in his voice. He said, in the same amiable tone, 'Yeah, great talking to you, man. Call sometimes, when you find the time. The way things are, who knows when one's number is up!'

'Anything you will say. Bye now. Stay well.'

Abheek sat numbly, staring at the phone. Malini waited eagerly, but he just couldn't bring himself to speak. Some time passed before she asked impatiently, 'Well, was it good to speak to him?'

'What? Yes, of course.'

He left it at that.

Through the day, Abheek felt strangely disturbed – as if a sore had opened up inside. While Malini cooked, he sat alone on the bedroom chaise longue with a book, not reading. His thoughts were transported to that time in

Kolkata, when he had practically shifted to Tivoli Court in the weeks leading up to the twelfth standard board exams. Chhaya Mashi, having somehow got it into her head that Bunty would fail the exams, had implored Abheek to come over and study with him. But Bunty couldn't care less about the ISC, his entire focus had shifted to the SATs. When confronted, he was quite short with his parents and strangely, they too, seemed wary of pushing him beyond a point. This surprised Abheek, as it was not how things worked in his house. Chhaya Mashi wanted Bunty to concentrate on the boards, because she didn't want him to leave for America at that age. Knowing Bunty, this apprehension was perfectly justified. She often asked why he couldn't choose a good college for a bachelor's course in the city, even promising that she would support him if he still wanted to go to the US later, for a postgraduate degree. As an incentive, she would offer, 'I'll talk to Anju Di, you and Bappa can live together in this house, through college. It will be like hostel life, with all the home comforts, how about that?' Bunty would only snigger derisively. He had started growing his hair, taking guitar lessons; in his mind, halfway gone.

Chhaya Mashi hadn't given up. She would often coax Abheek to work on his friend, dissuade him from the path he had set his heart on. Abheek promised to help, but did the opposite. If anything, he encouraged Bunty to focus on the SATs, helping out with the mock tests, spotting patterns in the previous year's exam sheets for him, even lying about their study sessions when quizzed by Bunty's parents. Later, he even worked on Bunty's admissions forms, wrote the essays. There could be no doubt, then or now, that he had wanted Bunty to go.

After Bunty got admission and left for America, Chhaya Mashi became a nervous wreck. Bunty's father asked Abheek to continue staying with them for a while, and he obliged happily. He attended college using the Tivoli Court house as a base, and was comfortable by all accounts. But as the weeks passed, he got tired of her constant whining, the rants against her husband for having paid the astronomical tuition fees and the frenzy of worry she whipped herself into if Bunty didn't call, however briefly, every weekend. He eventually returned home and told his family that it was because he couldn't suffer his friend's mother's tantrums anymore. Atreyi asked once if he ever felt bad – having egged Bunty on – to see her in this state, to which his reply was evasive.

As he reflected on that time now, her question came back to him and Abheek wondered, not for the first time, if it had been an accusation. For it was also around that time, when the distance between the two of them began to take root. It was plain to Abheek that his sister didn't think much of him, and he had a feeling it was his ambition, and self-absorption, that put her off. Had that impression been formed as early as that time in Kolkata? Did she also wonder, like him, what his real motivations may have been, in goading Bunty on? Had they really been purely unselfish – helping a friend realize a dream? He had never confronted that question himself over the years. It sat uneasily in his diary of life – an unsolved equation, abandoned.

There were moments that afternoon when Abheek wanted to pick up his phone and call Bunty. He was pulled by the prospect but also scared. He let it be. That is what he did – let things be, till they lost their urgency, dying a slow death.

Malini left him alone with his thoughts. It was demanding enough – bumping into each other all the time as they moved within the walls of the house, trying to fill the days.

It was only in the evening, as they sat with their first drink, that she thought she had given him enough time.

'Something is bothering you, Abheek, after you spoke to Bunty. Want to tell me about it?'

Abheek didn't pretend it was nothing. 'Yes. It's just that talking to him took me back to that time – it was an important time of my life, you know – and I haven't been able to shake it off.'

'Why would you want to shake it off, though? Are they unpleasant memories?'

'No. But complicated.'

A silence gathered. Malini broke it. 'Are his parents alive? Were you close to them?'

'Chhaya Mashi is, but Salil Mesho passed away. I didn't ask him when. That's when he must have returned to India.'

'Oh, I didn't know he stayed on in America all those years. Did you keep in touch? In the early years, I mean.'

A dampness began to gather in the folds of Abheek's neck.

'Yes, he wrote occasionally from there. I think he had some kind of job in shipping, but not sure. But, no, the correspondence didn't continue.'

'You mean, you didn't write back. God, you men are so strange. And is he married, any children?'

'I... I don't know. But he spoke only about his mother when I asked him about the folks at home, so I don't think...'

Malini dropped her hands to her side in exasperation. She gave him a withering look before stomping away to the kitchen. She returned with refills.

'What about his mother? Did you ever call to check on her?'

'I lived in that house for a while, even after Bunty had left. I was in touch with her, on and off. She began losing her mind though.'

Abheek's forehead was now sweating too. He rose unsteadily and rushed to the bathroom. There he stood, staring back at himself in the mirror – a dissembler's slyness in the red-rimmed eyes, not a face he would trust.

He hadn't told Malini the truth. After he packed his things and left, Chhaya Mashi had called Abheek, at a neighbour's where he could receive calls from friends. She was hysterical on the line – wailing, raving that Bunty had fallen into bad company and would end up ruining his future. Abheek had made some placatory noises – promising to come by – and ended the conversation. A few weeks later, to his utter surprise, Salil Mesho turned up at his college, asking for him. Abheek remembered that meeting vividly. It was the last time he saw Bunty's father. Hunched over a cup of tea, in that dingy canteen, he looked a wreck. Chhaya Mashi had developed psychiatric problems, he said. More alarmingly, he had received a call from the dean of the college in the US. Bunty had apparently dropped out. All his efforts to reach Bunty had been unfruitful. Salil Mesho confided that he had taken a very substantial loan from his company to pay for the course – it wasn't easy in those days to afford dollar tuitions. All he asked of Abheek was that he come and spend some time with Chhaya Mashi. She had always regarded him as a son and maybe his presence would make her feel better. Relations between Bunty's parents had soured to an extent where they were not on speaking terms. Salil Mesho didn't know who else to reach out to.

But Abheek never went to that house again. He also left instructions with his neighbour not to pass down calls from Bunty's parents. And then, he left for Bangalore for his post graduation, turning his back on the city for good. Had Atreyi really been that harsh in judging him?

Abheek looked away from the mirror, splashed water on his face and went back to the drawing room. He took a sip of beer and told Malini, 'You are right. I need to speak to Bunty again.'

'I'll leave you alone. Call me when you are done.'

A few moments later, Abheek was on the phone with Bunty.

'Abheek? What's the matter? Twice in a single day? Or did you press call by mistake?'

'No, no, Bunty. No mistake. Actually, I hung up abruptly in the morning, then realized I hadn't asked you many of the questions I intended to. Was just having a drink with Malini, thought I would try again.'

'Good, good. So, what are these questions, let me hear? Heh.'

'Uff, it's nothing like that. Stuff like when you came back from the US, whether you have a family…'

'I see. So, let me fill in the blanks. Baba passed away in August 2012, that's when I had to take a call. Ma couldn't be alone in Cal. I would have to either come back or take her there. I don't mind telling you – you are like family – she's been mentally ill for years now. To drag her across the seas at this age didn't seem right. Fran and I had separated long ago, so there weren't any other people to consider. It was my decision, and I took the plunge. You know better than most, how much I troubled her when I was a boy. Thought it was high time I made amends, haha.'

'Ah, so it's been eight years already, huh? And before that would you come down often to Kolkata?'

There was a moment's hesitation, before Bunty said, 'Not really. You see, Baba and I were not exactly on great terms; you can hardly blame him…'

'I see. And the restaurant?'

'You have not been to our house in Lansdowne Road, right? Of course, how could you, silly of me. It's nothing big, just a couple of rooms on top and what used to be a pharmacy at the ground level. My parents needed the income, so we rented it out. After my return, I worked for a year with an IT firm in Salt Lake, but you know how it is – after the US you can't take the work scene in bloody Kolkata. It wasn't for me. So, I poached the chef from a nearby Chinese restaurant, gave notice to the pharmacy guys and invested my meagre savings in setting up this small chow house there. Started slow, but it had begun picking up, till this bloody thing blew up in my face. Blame the lines on my forehead… my cursed luck!'

Bunty spoke so easily, as if no time had elapsed. Like it was usual for them to call each other often and chat for hours.

'What do you plan to do with the restaurant now? I mean if things continue this way…'

'You know me. I don't stress much about stuff, but this one has me worried. Thank God there is no rent to cover, but the salaries, my own running expenses, Ma's medical stuff… It's not as if I am loaded. My savings are down to zilch. I am almost hand to mouth.'

'Bunty, listen…' Abheek began, but couldn't finish. It just felt awkward. He decided he would write Bunty a note later.

Malini was hovering. Maybe it was time for dinner.

'Listen, we'll speak again soon. Okay? And when all this is over, maybe I'll come down and we can catch up over a drink, what do you say?'

'Done. And it will be at my restaurant, if that's still alive then. The chilli pork will kill you, I promise. We put a bit of that naga chilli in it… You will have fire coming out of your ears! Hahaha.'

After dinner, Abheek typed out a mail, offering Bunty a long-term loan of five lakhs, to tide over the crisis. He wrote in as gracious a tone as he could manage, conscious of how tricky it was to offer help to anyone. He reckoned the amount would be enough to see his friend through the next three months at least. If things didn't improve by then, all bets were off anyway.

He felt lighter, even slept better than he had of late.

When his eyes opened in the morning, Malini was still fast asleep, and Abheek tiptoed away to the sitting room to open his laptop. He logged on, and sure enough, there was a mail from Bunty.

It read:

Dear Abheek,

I cannot tell you how happy I was to receive your calls yesterday. You may think I am being sentimental, but I almost had tears in my eyes after we spoke in the evening. It made me feel so nostalgic about our school days.

Thank you for your very kind offer to help out, and I won't deny that the money would be a lifesaver at this point, but I won't be able to accept it, Abheek. Don't misunderstand, I know you offer it with the best intentions, but somehow, accepting will make me feel small. But the mere offer is worth many, many more millions to me, I promise you. I am very grateful.

I told Ma that you called and asked after her. Know what she said?

'Abheek? What did he call to say? Must have stood first in class again. What a bright boy!' Imagine.

Lots of love,
Your old friend.

~

8

The Stroll

Varun felt his knees wobble. He wondered if it was his imagination. He had barely made it to the leafy lane of the Campion School, weaving past the Oval Maidan, which couldn't be more than a mile from his residence. It was his first foray outside the house in over two months. Did it take only that long for the body – even one past its prime – to lose an age-old habit like walking? He hoped not, but noticed again something unsure about his stride, even a slight catch near the right side of his groin.

The guard at the building gate had been surprised to see him – it was usually Ramu, his live-in help, who came down nowadays to fetch the stuff Varun ordered online. This stroll had actually been Ramu's suggestion.

'*Saab*, it's been two months. Don't mind, but I think you may feel better if you walked around a bit. Some fresh air, sunshine…' he had advanced in a sheepish voice this morning. Maybe it was Ramu who needed some time to himself.

Come to think of it, it was surprising the nudge hadn't come sooner. Varun was taken aback at how quickly his reluctance to step outdoors had wormed itself in, till the very thought of going out stopped occurring to him altogether. Even when he stood on the third-floor balcony and looked out on to the maidan, the empty streets below didn't look inviting enough. There was no pressing need to go out, of course. For the last two decades, he had worked from home, pegging away at his books on his desktop. He lived alone, having never married; Ramu had been his sole companion since he moved into this apartment – bequeathed to him by his mother over 12 years ago. His material needs were simple, nothing that required him to venture out personally; one could say that about other needs too, particularly of the social variety. Perhaps it was this solitary lifestyle which vexed Ramu, more than the lack of air and sunlight.

It wasn't that Varun was sedentary by nature, far from it. Till the announcement of the lockdown, his morning routine included two full laps around the Oval Maidan and he always looked forward to it. There had been plays and concerts at the neighbouring NCPA which lured him out of his lair, as did the weekly visit to the book store in Fort. But that was it, really. He wasn't too keen on dining out alone. Ramu's simple home-cooked meals were adequate for him. Friends had come and gone over the years; now it all seemed too much of an effort. He did notice the bafflement in Ramu's eyes – how does this man manage to live inside his head all day? – and while he understood, he didn't feel the need to justify his aloof nature.

Varun may have continued with his morning walks, had it not been for that brush with the policeman on the very first day of the lockdown. The man had stopped him on the pavement right outside his building and said, firmly though not discourteously, 'People of your age are advised to stay indoors, sir. Please abide by the rules, unless it is for essential items, or a medical emergency.'

Varun had considered saying he was on his way to the market, but had turned back. And that was that – what followed was two months of self-imposed house arrest.

The knees notwithstanding, he couldn't deny that it was good to be out. For one, the city resembled those black and white photographs – taken in the fifties – he had purchased from the Phillips antique shop further down the road. Practically no traffic, very few pedestrians, just those grand old buildings around the maidan, the Cooperage park, statues on the islands between roads – old Bombay, of which one could still catch a fleeting glimpse sometimes on a lazy Sunday afternoon. He hoped someone was clicking images now, for posterity – a city returned to its former charm by a fearful contagion.

Varun decided to give his legs a proper workout, now that he had bothered to step out. He charted a route in his head – a left on to the causeway, all the way down the street to the temple opposite the cake shop, turning into the road that led to the Colaba market. If it was open, he would surprise Jayshree – his regular *fishwali* – and pick up some pomfret perhaps; it had been a while since he had had a good fish curry. He would then take the Mereweather Road on his way back, turning right into the seafront promenade, past the Taj Mahal Palace hotel, the Yacht Club, up to the Regal cinema circle, and then cut through the maidan to his building. That would be enough for the day. Any more and he may need to summon Ramu to carry him back on his shoulders.

By the time he mapped this out, his steps had led him to the causeway. If the emptiness of the roads outside his house, so many weeks into the ban, had come as a surprise to Varun, what he saw now stunned him. He had had the impression that shops had been allowed to reopen and expected to see some of them open for custom, but the usually pulsating causeway resembled a desolate cemetery, the nameplates on the shops, its tombstones. Not a single shutter was up, no hawker in sight, only a handful of pedestrians in masks walked listlessly with shopping bags in hand. If he had been happy to see empty roads earlier, this sight sank his spirits. How could Colaba Causeway be like this? All those reports he read every day, about the plight of small businessmen and their employees, suddenly became more real. Where had the hawkers gone – would they reappear miraculously the day an all clear was sounded, or had they abandoned the city of their dreams? How many of these pavement shops would never open again?

He saw a small group of women and children squatting in one of the bylanes.

One of them looked up hopefully and asked, 'You've brought food?'

He shook his head, realizing that local residents were probably providing meals to them, hence the expectation – he thought of giving them some money, but none of them wore masks, and he felt unsure about approaching them. He walked on, almost unconsciously bracing for the whiff of roasting meat outside Café Churchill, but of course the restaurant was firmly shut. Yet smell, too, invoked a memory of its own, did it not?

The street remained deserted till he had reached the turn that led to the Colaba market. He gazed wistfully in the direction of Theobroma, the pastry shop, and felt a pang again. How well the enterprising Parsi sisters had done – the pink and green of the shopfront reminded him of his last visit to the bookshop. The owner had been placing copies of a new book, about the Theobroma story, on the display window when he walked in. He hoped the shop would open soon. More immediately, he felt the urge to rush in, buy their brownies and *mawa* cakes to carry back home, maybe even give some to the group he passed on the road. There were hungry children there.

His thoughts were interrupted by the clanging of bells. Varun wheeled around in surprise, but the gates of the temple, next to which he stood, were firmly locked. Even the plump cow devotees fed grass to – a fixture outside the entrance – was missing. The ringing continued though, he hadn't imagined it. Varun tried conjuring up an image, of a solitary priest seated in prayer, oblivious to the world outside, but it didn't ring true. Some back-door entry must have been allowed; the temple was a place of transaction, not mere worship.

On turning into the lane that led to the market, he sensed that it might be open. A trickle of people walked past, even some on bicycles who looked like they were carrying stuff for delivery. He asked one of them if the shops were open and the man gave him a nod of assurance. The fish market was open but defied the cliché of one – it could as easily have been a church – there was pin-drop silence. Three women sat in separate corners, all with forlorn expressions. Till Jayshree spotted Varun at the entrance and shouted, '*Arrey, babuji*! Come, come.'

He could have been a hero, returning victorious from some great endeavour, such was the welcome in her voice. Even the others, who didn't know him that well, extended their greetings.

'I didn't expect the market to be open. How are things, Jayshree?' Varun asked.

'Don't ask, *babuji*. Sometimes these guys open it, sometimes they don't. We have no say,' she said, pointing to a police van parked outside.

Two cops sat on plastic chairs, keeping an eye on what was now their domain. It wasn't difficult to surmise what was going on – people in any position of power in this country didn't need an invitation to exploit an opportunity. This one was out on a platter... poor vegetable vendors, fishmongers, storekeepers – desperate to conduct some – or any – business to stay afloat – easy pickings for policemen, municipal authorities.

Varun asked, 'Asking for bribes, are they?'

'What else? They get away with it with the vegetable vendors, not us. We are locals, they can't bully us that easily.'

Varun nodded. These fish-sellers were no pushovers; all Koli women with strong community networks. The others in the market came from all over – Bihar, UP, Rajasthan, and were easier to fleece.

'Is Anil still around?' he asked Jayshree, referring to his usual vegetable supplier. Before all this happened, Varun would drop in once a week, for the fish, and what Anil called Chinese vegetables – an avocado, some bell peppers, *pokchoi*, a sprig of basil or lime leaf. The material for Ramu's initiation into the world of non-Indian cuisine. Varun knew all of this could be ordered online, or fetched by

Ramu, but there was something about a vibrant marketplace which he had always found attractive. He was drawn to the banter between the vendors. Once, after a lady had paid 1,000 rupees for two avocados and a bunch of out-of-season asparagus stems, he overheard one of the lads in the shop tell the other, 'Ever tried eating that stuff, Manua?'

'Why, do I look crazy to you? In our village, even the cows would spit it out!'

'Haha. Yet, look at them – ready to buy at any price.'

'It's because of the price, duffer. From tomorrow, start selling *tinda* at 200 a kilo, and they will become interested.'

As a writer, where else could Varun hope to find such priceless material?

Jayshree made a face. 'No, *babuji*. I don't see Anil around. A month ago, I spoke to him briefly – he said he was going through a tough time and borrowed a few hundred rupees from me. That's alright, but I haven't seen him since.'

'And Salim, the *fruitwala*?'

'Gone. You will find one or two guys outside, selling stuff. They are from the slum nearby. The rest are gone.'

Varun wanted to turn and walk away. He felt he shouldn't have come down at all. But now, he couldn't leave without buying something. There were prawns and pomfret on the counter and he asked for some. He pointed to the ladyfish too, but Jayshree said, under her breath, without looking up, '*Babuji*, don't mind, but why don't you buy something from them too? They haven't had a customer all morning.'

'Of course,' Varun said and walked across to the other women. He bought little bits from both, they thanked him for doing a *bauni* – first purchase – from them. He felt better.

He had half a mind to accost the two policemen and ask them why they were needling the local vendors, but decided not to. He walked out from the other entrance. By this time, the sun was sharp and he felt drained. The thought of lugging the bag, though it wasn't too heavy, all the way back, seemed daunting. He resolved to start his morning walks again. No way was he about to let this virus turn him into a housebound vegetable.

By the time Varun reached the mouth of Mereweather Road, the number of pedestrians had thinned again. Turning the corner, he could see the entire stretch of road ahead – all the way up to the back wall of the Yacht Club – without a single person on it. It was a lovely shaded lane, deserted – a solitary street dog asleep in the middle – as far as the eye could see. Beautiful, but eerie.

Varun paused near the small community park, hoping to find *jamuns* strewn on the footpath. There were none, it wasn't time yet. The *jamun* season was so short, but one of these days, soon enough, the street corner would be purple with their crushed skin. The sprawling tree which bore them was itself quite grand; he had missed it. These were his friends, whereas human company he found grossly overrated.

A strange thought occurred to him – how many *jamun* seasons did he have left? It brought a smile to his face – this idea of measuring, so, what remained of his life.

Varun was ambling slowly, staring at the facades of elegant, old buildings like Fosbery House, feeling transported in time, when he suddenly heard voices. Three young men, handkerchiefs tied around their mouths, emerged from one of the lanes connecting the road to the causeway. They stopped walking upon seeing Varun. Both parties stood still, assessing each other. There was no reason to, but he felt uneasy.

The men came closer.

'You live nearby?' one of them asked.

'Yes, why?'

'Just asking. Went to the market?'

Varun nodded. The other two boys were glancing up and down the road.

'Can you give us some money? We haven't eaten since yesterday.'

'What do you have in the bag? Any bread, biscuits?'

Varun stepped back. Something in their voices made him wary.

'It's just fish, nothing you can eat like that. I am sorry to hear…'

'Give us some money then.' This was no request.

Varun looked down the road. There wasn't a soul in sight. He took his wallet out.

'Let me give you a couple of hundred rupees. The market is open, you will find food there…'

Before he could finish, one of the boys snatched the wallet away from him; the grasping hand, Varun noticed, had bright red polish on the overgrown nail of its little finger. Odd, the images that stick in moments of shock.

'Listen, this isn't…'

'Just walk away, uncle. We won't hurt you. Where's your phone?'

'I am not carrying it, it's at home.'

The boy walked up and patted Varun down. Not finding anything but the house keys, he shoved Varun. Varun took a step back to balance himself but his heel landed on the edge of the kerb and he toppled over backwards, bag spinning out of his hand, fish spilling out from the plastic packets on to the footpath.

'Run!' one of them shouted, and they scampered away, down the lane back towards the causeway.

Varun lay there, supporting himself on his elbows, more stunned than injured. His ankle throbbed. On sitting up, he saw that his left elbow was scraped and there was a little blood. Other than that, he was not hurt. The pounding inside his chest was easing slowly. The air was full of the cawing of crows, many of them swirling agitatedly above his head, some hopping around on the sidewalk trying to get close to the spilt fish. He sat, hands around his knees, staring at the empty lane. A car sped past on the adjacent road, towards the seafront, too quickly for the driver to notice him sitting there.

He thought of walking down the causeway to the Colaba police *chowki*. His debit and PAN cards were in the wallet, he would need to report the incident. He stood up gingerly, wincing at the pain in his leg. The ankle would need tending to. He looked at the bag, wondering what to do with it. The crows had started picking out the silverfish by now. Varun shooed them away and retrieved the small bags which hadn't burst. He put the parcels inside the larger bag and placed it on a wall by the gate of a house, hoping someone would find it. He didn't have the strength to carry it back now.

He hobbled on, trying to put as little weight on the injured ankle as possible, somehow managing to cover the short distance to the station. A guard at the station gate spotted him and ran over.

'What happened, sir?'

'Ah, an accident. I need to file a report.'

The man extended a hand to support him, but Varun waved it away with a smile.

Inside, he was ushered to a table, where an inspector sat poring over files. Seeing Varun, he put on his mask hastily.

'What exactly happened?'

'I was walking back from the Colaba market with a bag of fish, when I had a sudden turn – must have been the heat – and fainted on the pavement.'

Varun showed the inspector his elbow and told him about the ankle.

'Oh.'

The inspector looked puzzled; had he come to report a blackout?

'I don't know how long I was out, couldn't have been more than a few minutes, but when I came to, I realized my wallet was gone.'

'You are sure about it?'

'Of course. I used it at the market. There wasn't a lot of cash, maybe a couple of thousand, but it had all my identification cards, bank cards too.'

'PAN and Aadhaar both?'

'And my election card.'

'Do you remember any of the numbers?'

Varun gave him the PAN number, the only one he knew by heart, and promised to message him the rest.

'Did you sense that someone was trying to remove the wallet from your pocket?'

'No, I was passed out. Only realized it when I stood up again.'

The inspector looked up at the guard who had escorted him in.

'This is the reason we have all these patrol vans posted everywhere. The roads are so empty, these mischief makers can sense an opportunity any time.'

'People are distressed. They are hungry. I don't blame them,' Varun offered.

The inspector glared at him.

'Well, if you knew all that sir, was it wise to step out on your own? Surely someone else can do your errands for you, no?' he said, looking Varun up and down, as if to gauge his economic station. Resident of a posh locality, retired and comfortable – he may have concluded.

'If you hadn't, you would have been safe, saved us some hassle.'

'Lesson learnt, officer. Henceforth, I shall remember.'

This seemed to mollify the man.

'Arrey, sir, don't take it like that. This is a difficult time for everyone. We are also very thinly stretched. Can I offer you some tea?'

'No, thank you. But if one of your jeeps can drop me home… It's just opposite the Oval Maidan.'

'Of course.' He signalled to the guard to arrange one.

'I'll also ask the guys on patrol to check around the area. It's a wallet so I am not too hopeful, but you never know. Please block the cards the moment you reach home.'

Varun thanked him and walked to the jeep which was waiting at the gate. Seated inside, he thought about the report he had filed, recalled the flash of the red nail polish. Not snatching the wallet from his hand, but plucking away black leaves from a bunch of basil, weighing bell peppers on a scale for him.

9

Homecoming

Long queues still reminded me of the cloudburst which ravaged our state a few years ago, when everyone in the village had gathered – as relief arrived – to collect rations. The numbers today on the railway platform where Mohan Da and I stood, were much larger – there must have been at least a thousand of us, in a line that began at one end of the station and spilled over to the street on the other end of the platform.

Cops wielded batons to ensure we were three feet apart. Like the others, I seethed inside for what we had been made to endure over the last month. It wasn't fear but hope that kept us from lashing out. None of us spoke. Only they did, barking the same orders again and again – don't come closer, keep your masks on, don't touch anyone, step on to the bogies on being told, always maintain a single file. I carried a rucksack, which had my clothes and a bag they had given me outside, containing food and water for the journey. After six weeks of waiting, I was finally going home.

Once boarding started and we reached the sixth wagon, my heart began to beat faster – there were still so many in the queue ahead of me. They were allowing only a few people into each compartment, perhaps so we could still be three feet apart, inside. What if the train filled up before my turn came? But I didn't have to wait long. Soon I heard a 'chalo' from the policeman next to me and I clambered into the train without touching the handrail at the entrance. The sleeper berths were all opened out. Someone said that we were to lie down in individual bunks, one to each. No more than two could sit on the lower berth, one on either end.

I whispered to Mohan Da, 'I'll climb to the top berth, Mohan Da. You take the lower one here, okay? When I get tired of lying down, I will come down and you go up.'

'No, let me go up first. You sit by the window. Later, once the train starts, I will come down.'

I nodded and quickly took the window seat. All the tension had made me want to go to the toilet badly, but I didn't want to lose the seat. Outside, the queue on the platform had vanished; they must have asked the exact number of passengers to come to the station.

I marvelled at how organized it all was. So many people but no jostling or screaming. Everyone had masks on and were given provisions for the journey. And then the anger returned – if they could do it so easily, why hadn't they done it earlier? Why did they have to put us through so much misery?

Anyway, there was a loud whistle and the train started moving with a jerk. There was some clapping from inside. One of the cops on the platform shouted to another, '*Saala*, look at them. Going home to starve but behaving as if they are off on some vacation! *Gandus*.'

I wanted to shout back, ask what it was to his father even if that were true, but checked myself. After all, I was heading home.

Once the train left the station, I thought everyone would mill around, throwing caution to the winds, but they did not. At first, I imagined it was because of the guard posted in each compartment, but that wasn't it. The weeks gone by had made of us a herd of cattle – timid, submissive creatures with hunger in our eyes, ready to fall in line with any command or rebuke – as if the life had been sucked out of us. I just want to die at home, someone had said at the camp, and we looked at him as if he had spoken for all of us.

Before boarding, we were all asked if we had a cough or fever, our temperatures checked. Most of us were let through, only a handful asked to step aside. I felt a wave of relief when I was waved through; also because I didn't have the disease, though Mohan Da said that it didn't prove anything – you could not have fever yet be sick inside. I was going to ask what difference it made as long as I didn't suffer, but realized that I could make others sick in a way that was worse. How unfair that would be, I thought, if someone else caught it from me and died, while I remained fine.

A man walked up and asked, 'Mind if I sit down?'

'Feel free. What's the point of this three feet distance now? For one and a half months, we were sleeping practically on top of each other, right? Whatever had to happen has already happened,' I said.

'I was also thinking of that. So, where is home for you?'

'Near Almora. And you?'

'Lalkuan.'

'Oh, but will the train stop there? Heard it was non-stop; maybe you will have to walk back from Haldwani.'

'Maybe. No problem. What's a few miles of walking these days? Everyone seems to be on their way somewhere.'

The man had a gentle way of talking. His name was Dheeru, he said.

Mohan Da had been lying with his head propped up on his elbow, listening to the conversation. He leaned forward and asked, 'Where did you work? Did you get paid your dues?'

Dheeru's pained expression said everything Mohan Da needed to know.

It took me back to that morning, when the nightmare began. It was the crack of dawn. Mohan Da and I were fast asleep on tables at the highway dhaba where we worked. Manohar Seth woke us rudely by splashing cold water on our faces. We thought there was a fire or something like that, but Seth said, 'They are shutting everything down. Get your things and come out immediately.'

Noticing our blank expressions, he explained, 'It's the disease which has been spreading. Apparently it is now an epidemic, like a plague, and the government is closing everything down. The order came last night. Get ready, quickly!'

Outside, he gave us 2,000 rupees each.

'This is all I have. Now, run to the toll *naka*. Maybe you will be lucky and manage to get on the last bus. Trains are shut already.'

Mohan Da asked about the money Seth had promised to hold for him. This was a usual practice for both of us. It ensured we had a kitty to take back home. Seth had at least 30,000 of his and a similar amount of mine.

Seth gaped at Mohan Da, as if he had said something ludicrous. 'How will I get hold of that now? Take it when you are back, I won't steal it, you know. Now go, or else you will have to walk back to Uttarakhand from here.'

I looked around for Gopi and Lakshman, our other colleagues, but couldn't see them.

'They left a while ago,' said Seth, pointing in the other direction, the way to the Maharashtra border.

I asked, 'Seth, will you call us when everything is alright again?'

'Of course, how else will I reopen the dhaba? But don't turn up on your own, before I give you the go ahead. Now leave.'

It all became a blur after that; days blending into nights, one meal a day if we were lucky, staring into one another's hollow eyes. Mercifully, it wasn't the peak of summer.

Otherwise we would have perished on the way. Later, there was refuge – we were herded into makeshift tents on a field. Airless and filthy, the food inedible. We waited, like animals in a slaughterhouse. There were rumours that they would put us to work on highway construction sites, but that didn't materialize. The money would have been useful, but secretly I was happy it didn't. All I wanted was to be back in Almora. It was this foolish ambition, to earn a better living, that had landed me in this soup – a lesson never to be forgotten.

The morning we set out, I had called home and spoken to my father. Days later, I begged one of the camp guards to let me make a 10-second call. I managed to say hello to my wife, tell her that I was alive and would be home soon. She wept loudly on hearing my voice, but couldn't say much more in that short time.

And then one day, we heard that trains had been arranged to take us back to our states. By then, we didn't even have the energy to feel happy. Many in our group were doubtful, fearing it was another empty promise. But here we were, sitting in trains, homeward bound.

I stared out of the window, happy with how fast the train was moving. Even if it stopped – for some reason – before reaching our final destination, we would still have covered quite a bit of the way home. That was not nothing.

Mohan Da climbed down from his berth and sat next to me. As if by tacit understanding, the guy who had been sitting with me on the lower berth now took his place there. We opened our bags and took out some rotis wrapped in foil, wondering if we should keep some for later, but Dheeru had heard that a meal would be served on the train at night, so we ate them all.

'What will you do when you get back?' Dheeru asked as we ate.

'First, I will have a bath, then eat a mound of rice and sleep for two days on a proper bed. After that, we will see.'

Mohan Da laughed. It was so nice to hear the sound of it, after long. 'I don't think he was asking about that, but what you would do for a living,' he said.

'What is there to do, Mohan Da? Isn't that the reason we came away in the first place? But this time, I'll have to think hard about it. Even if this disease goes away, and Seth calls us back, I have to decide if it is worth it. Two thousand in Almora may be better than 12,000 in Gujarat.'

'Is it, I wonder?'

The way Mohan Da said that gave me pause. In a way he was right, the money I earned there did mean a lot. I couldn't deny it helped me dream bigger.

'And you'll let the money with Seth go?'

'I know. That's the hook he retained, in case he needs us back,' I said, wishing we had pressed him harder for our money. In that panic and confusion, we had left without thinking things through. As Seth might have thought we would.

Having eaten, we lay down in our individual bunks. From time to time, one of us tried to strike up a conversation, but couldn't really sustain one. What did one talk about but the past or the future? One held trauma, the other uncertainty. It was better to try and sleep, repair some of the fatigue accumulated in our worn-out bodies. The gentle rolling of the train was like a balm for my wrecked back and bruised feet. I drifted in and out of sleep, half dreaming about being back home, playing with Sonu and Titli, watching Gauri make hot rotis for me on the *chulha*, smiling slyly.

Time passed slowly. But I was used to it by now. At first, I would feel restless, sitting idly in the shelter with nothing to do; every hour felt like a whole day. Sometimes, when I thought I would go mad, I would badger Mohan Da to get up and start walking again. But as the days passed, I fell into a lifeless swoon, losing all track of time. I knew it was a kind of illness; it didn't feel right.

Lying down on the berth now, watching the world rush past – this was easier; at least there was a sense of movement. It was only Dheeru's question that filled me with gloom. Earlier, I may have deflected it, thinking I would cross that bridge when I came to it, but now with every leap of the train, the problem came closer. It was one, I realized, that would follow me forever; appearing, at times, to get better before something went wrong again.

I remembered my father's words the day I told him of my decision to leave the village in search of work. The city was like a giant sugarcane crusher, he said. It would squeeze me dry and spit me out. How prophetic his warning had been. I only hoped he wouldn't remind me of it. He wasn't an unkind man; besides, in his time, he had tried as well, first as a small truck driver in Rudrapur and then at the sugar factory in Simbhaoli. But he had come back to the village after each of these stints. Now, he was a brooding man who sat on a charpoy and said things like, 'It's good to try, but you will die as you were born. It's not possible to change much in one lifetime.'

I remembered him drawing a circle on the mud courtyard with his stick as he said this, knocking the tip at the point where the circle began, and ended. At the shelter, I thought of him often – with affection, never out of fear of his ridicule. It was good that Mohan Da was always next to me, else I would have felt very alone.

A song drifted in from another cabin. It was from someone's phone. I thought of walking up and requesting him to let me make a call home, but decided not to. It was a matter of a few more hours anyway. Scattered pieces of conversation floated in, on and off, but on the whole, the compartment was quiet. Either the men were all exhausted from their ordeal, or, like me, solemn in contemplation of what lay ahead. Their relief at boarding the train would have given way to worry, just as mine had. It struck me then that I hadn't seen a single woman at the station. What happened to all the women from construction sites? Were they all locals, I wondered. No, I had seen Nepali women there; though it was true that I didn't know even one girl from our own area who had gone to the city in search of work.

The train slowed down before reaching Haldwani. Looking out, I saw lots of people, mainly boys and men, running towards us. I realized it must be the first train they were seeing in over a month. By the tracks, women sat outside their shanties and gaped, as if we were aliens arriving from some other planet. Something about the way they stared made me put my mask on again. None of them wore masks, maybe the disease wasn't such a big issue in these parts. One young boy picked up a stone and hurled it at the train; it bounced off the metal carriage.

The guard came by to say that the train would be reaching soon. We were to remain seated till he asked us to walk out, four at a time. By now, we knew the drill. As the train ground to a halt, I peered outside the window to see quite a reception. The platform looked like a hospital – people dressed in white overalls and proper masks stood in a line with temperature guns. We were to be tested again.

'They can't take chances. On the other side, it was easy; they would have been happy just to see our backs, but here it is their own state. One sick person could create big trouble,' Mohan Da said.

He always knew when I found something perplexing, explaining it before I had to ask.

I could see buses lined up on the road outside. When the first batch of passengers stepped off the train, they were made to stand in front of the officials who would be testing them. Questions were asked, their temperatures taken. Each was handed a packet before being herded out of the station. I was very impressed. Those fancy states should take a leaf out of our humble mofussil, I told Mohan Da, not without pride.

Once we were done with the test, the three of us walked outside. A uniformed policeman asked us our destination and pointed the two of us to a blue bus which said Bageshwar in front.

I turned to Dheeru and said, 'Okay, *bhaiya*, have a safe ride back home. Heaven knows if we will meet again, but take care of yourself.'

'And don't fret about work and money. Something will work out. You are alive and healthy, that's more important,' Mohan Da added.

Dheeru smiled and walked away. He looked sad at parting with us.

The buses departed one after the other. Each of us had an entire seat to ourselves. The station had been crowded, but outside, the roads were empty and shops shut. As the bus started climbing up the winding road, I looked down at the snaking river, the green hillside, and felt my spirits lift. A cold draft blew in through the open window and I dozed off.

I slept practically all the way up. Each time the bus lurched and my eyes opened for a moment, I felt happier, as if each bend on the road healed something inside me. Once, I turned to see Mohan Da lying down on the seat with his legs propped up against the window, feet dangling outside in the breeze. A bell tinkled. I recognized the sound – we must have passed a Golu mandir by the roadside. My eyes shut again slowly.

Eventually, Mohan Da poked me in the ribs and said, 'Get up now. We are in Almora. Ask the driver if he will drop you off higher up on the road or if you should get off here and walk.'

The driver said that if he started going out of his way for every passenger, there would be too many stops. But he knew the area and agreed to drop a few of us together at a point where the walk to the village would be no more than an hour or so.

Mohan Da decided he would get off at the stop after mine, as Sunauli, his village, was further away.

He told me, 'Recharge your phone here. I'll call. And remember the instructions – no hugging people on reaching home, even the children. Keep a distance for the next two weeks.'

Mohan Da waved from the window as the bus moved away, and my eyes filled with tears. He was only going to the next village, but even so.

On the way to Basoli, I met very few people. I had taken my mask off, and no one looked at me with any curiosity. As I approached the village, I decided to cover my face again; the testers at the station had specifically asked us to. Basoli looked the same – a tiny hamlet of a hundred houses, more women than men. The men had all gone to the city for work, or joined the army. Now many of them, like me, would be coming back.

My first stop was the *gram pradhan's* house. I shouted his name and he emerged at the door. He didn't greet me, hesitating at first. I realized I had the mask on.

When I lowered it, he said, 'Oh, it's you.'

Usually, he would say something more to welcome me. Perhaps ask about the state of the cities or how long I was back for, but today he seemed distant.

'Someone came by from the DM's office the other day, to say that 10-12 of you would be returning by train. I was told to ensure that you don't mingle with the rest of the villagers for some time, and report to the police if you do.

I hope I won't have to. Now go home, and stay there till it's safe for you to come out.'

He shook his head, as if in disapproval, and went back inside. I walked away, feeling heavier than before.

I passed my friend Bhuwan's house; Chhotu, his little boy, sat outside with his dog. I waved at him but instead of waving back, he turned his lips and started whimpering. Maybe the mask scared him. Bhuwan's wife appeared and greeted me with a curt namaste, picked the boy up and went inside.

Otherwise, Basoli seemed normal. The two village shops were open, people sat around drinking tea. I didn't stop to chat with anyone, fearing I wouldn't be welcome, and headed for my house. I could feel their eyes on my back. I had called my father from Almora, and my family was expecting me.

There they stood, Gauri with Sonu and Titli clinging to her sides, my father standing further away. My wife had a wide smile on her face, which I was thankful for, and she wiped her eyes with the corner of her saree. Sonu looked like he wasn't sure if he should run into my arms or stay where he was.

First, I turned to my father and made a gesture of touching his feet, albeit from a distance.

It felt odd, almost as if I were seeking my own blessings, and I began to explain, but he said, 'It's not necessary. We know about it. Someone came and told us the other day. You can take my cot while you are here.'

We lived in a modest house with two small rooms. My father lived in the smaller room, which barely accommodated the cot he slept on. The four of us slept in the larger room, where we also cooked and ate. The pukka toilet outside was a more recent addition; I had got it built the last time I was home. Gauri and I had spoken about getting started on another room with the money I was supposed to bring home this time – the children were getting older, we needed our privacy – but that would have to wait now.

'No, Babuji, that won't be necessary. It's better if I sleep outside in the courtyard for a few days. It isn't cold any more and will be nice to lie under the open sky.'

'Yes. Where would you have found such skies in the city?' said Babuji with a knowing smile. The matter of sleeping arrangements was settled.

'How is your health? No difficulties, I hope?' Gauri asked in a low voice. She always spoke softly in my father's presence.

'No, I am fine. The last few days were very difficult, but I managed to get back in one piece. Still, it's best if I kept my distance from you all, at least for a week. Sonu, Titli, we can chat, but I will only be able to take you in my arms after a few days, okay? That way, whatever little chance there may be of you falling ill will be gone. Understood?'

They nodded.

Sonu lisped, 'But you don't look ill, *babuji*.'

'Yes, and I am not. This is just a precaution.'

'You didn't even get *mithai*?' accused Titli.

Babuji intervened. 'You must be hungry. Bahu, should he keep fielding questions from these two or will you give him something to eat?'

Gauri looked sheepish and ran back inside. She returned with plates, and we settled down in a circle; I sat a little farther away. There was rice, yellow dal and a green leaf bhaji, the best food I had had in weeks. Mohan Da dished out decent enough meals at the dhaba, but used more oil and spices than necessary. There was nothing like the simplicity of a home-cooked meal. At the end, there was some kheer – my favourite. Gauri gave Babuji a bowl of kheer with no sugar.

He said, 'Kheer without sweetness, what's the point? Anyway, you eat well. You look thinner. I am not surprised.'

'I haven't come back with much this time, Babuji. When the lockdown happened, Seth told us to run and he didn't clear our dues...'

'What else would you expect? He is a seth, right? Never mind; the key thing is you are back safely. I was speaking to the *pradhan* yesterday and he said there will be NREGA work starting soon, as we have no cases in this area. Two hundred rupees a day, that's not nothing, if you get even 10 days of work in a month. We won't starve. After that, we'll see.'

I saw Gauri nodding and felt stronger. Lately, I had begun feeling like I had let my family down, but now, after seeing how happy they were to have me back, that apprehension seemed misplaced. Together we would manage to tide over this difficult phase.

'Tulsi was saying we have received 500 in our bank account; I can go get it from Almora one day,' said Gauri.

Babuji gave her an indulgent smile and said, 'That is another project, bahu. You will have to stand in line all day for that. God knows how many women will be queuing up.'

'Still, it is something. And I can pitch for NREGA work as well...'

'Why? Before all that, we should use up my savings, right? If they don't come in handy at a time like this, what good is it?'

Babuji did have some money in his *grameen* bank account, seventy odd thousand the last time I had his passbook updated. Every other month, he would withdraw a little and buy something for the house, though I always asked him to save the money for a bad day. Since I started working in the city, there was never any need for him to contribute. Besides, I wanted him to have some money of his own, so that he never felt he was a burden on me. It also provided him with an excuse for a day out; he would make quite a show of setting out for Almora, saying to Gauri, 'Bahu, I have some work in the bank today. Will be evening by the time I get back.' Gauri never mentioned anything, but I suspect on those days he also had a tipple with his Almora friends on the way back. Otherwise, he didn't touch the stuff.

After the meal, I sat in the sun with Sonu and Titli and asked them what they had been up to while I was gone. They chattered away; I didn't register half the things they said, but the sing-song lilt of their voices soothed my ears. Gauri sat with a vessel of rice, sifting it for pieces of stone. There wasn't much to do, from what I could see; she just wanted to sit close to me and the kids. Her eyes told me she was hungry for my touch, but that would have to wait.

Usually, within minutes of my arrival, word would reach our neighbours, and they would drop in to ask after me. There were only so many of us here, we had grown up in each other's homes. The elders were like my parents, the men brothers. But today, as the sun slid behind the hill over Basoli, not a single visitor came.

Gauri noticed my eyes darting in the direction of the village and said, 'Don't make anything of it. They were told to keep away for a few days.'

The air was clear, the Nanda Devi golden in the setting sun; it made me feel the world would be fine again. I asked Gauri to step out of the room and went in to fetch my cot. After a while, my father brought his blue plastic chair out and sat near me.

'Get a shawl, you have just come up from the plains today,' he said.

As the sky darkened, Gauri came out and gave my father a lit hookah. He pulled on it and said, 'The hills are clean of it. There were a few cases in Haldwani – that too because of those *Tablighis* – but up here, nothing at all. It's just as well you had to come back. I was getting worried.'

'Yes, Babuji. I am not sure I will ever want to go back.'

Babuji didn't say anything for a while, and I was grateful for his silence. I sat with my head bowed for not having heeded his voice of experience. He could have rubbed it in, but only said, 'In a way, I am glad you went though.'

'How so?' I asked, surprised.

'Because if you hadn't, you would have always wondered what could have been – the opportunity you passed up. That regret would have made you bitter. It's better to have seen it for what it is. I took the same knocks myself, before being cured, of the lure of the big city.'

It wasn't the first time he mentioned the past, but we had never really had a frank discussion about it.

'When did you finally decide to return for good, Babuji?'

'The day I realized I was completely dispensable. I worked for someone for six years, then one day he said, over some small matter, "I can kick you out tomorrow and there will be a dozen people waiting outside to take your place at half your salary…" All the years counted for nothing. Workers like us, we are helpless.'

I felt an anger rising in me, against someone – Seth, the sugar factory owner who chucked Babuji out, the people who announced the shutdown without thinking about us once – who knows.

Babuji was saying, 'Till the day there are so many of us, poor and hungry, this won't change. They will always know they can throw us out at will, as millions more are waiting in the wings. As long as it serves them, they keep us; the moment something goes wrong, like now, we see their true colours.'

I had never heard Babuji sound so bitter. Maybe he felt angrier at my plight than he may have at his own.

'You are right, Babuji. I was telling Mohan Da on the train, it's better to be among your own even if it means earning a few rupees less.'

'At the end of the day, it is about dignity, beta. As long as you don't go hungry, that is the biggest thing. But yes, that much we have to organize somehow. Because it is easy to say that dal-roti will never be a problem, but it can be.'

Babuji's words brought back my fears again.

That night, once everyone had gone to sleep, I lay on the cot staring at the stars. I thanked God for giving me such a caring family, who didn't judge me for my mistakes or hold back their warmth because I had returned empty-handed. I tried to think positively about the possibilities

I could explore once my quarantine was over. It didn't take long for me to give up. After all, I knew these lands all too well – Basoli, Sunauli, Almora – there was very little work going around. Maybe a bit in the summer months, around Binsar or Kasar Devi, but hardly enough. And now, with the hotel trade down in the dumps, even less. Fewer plots of land would sell, new house construction would slow down to a trickle. If we had some land, I could try growing something, but our three *naalis* had just enough space for the rooms and a patch of vegetables. I had been thinking of buying a couple of cows, making a small shed for them with mud and stone... Babuji and Gauri could look after them and their milk could be a source of income for the family. All these little improvements which my savings would have made possible, now had to be shelved. I looked down, almost fearing I would see the circle Babuji had drawn in the ground. Then I fell into a deep slumber.

The next thing I knew, the sun was shining in my face and Titli was tying my ankles together with a piece of string, with meticulous care. I forgot the restrictions for a moment, and was about to pull her over when it struck me.

Keeping my voice down, I said, 'Titli! What are you doing? You aren't supposed to come near me. Go inside now, before your mother spanks you.'

She dropped the string and ran away. I felt I could have been gentler with her. Poor child, what was her fault?

Gauri emerged from the house with a glass of tea for me.

'Have a bath in the morning. The ASHA girl will come to see you today.'

'I see. The same one who…'

'Yes, Seema, who helped with Titli. She came yesterday to tell us that you needed to be checked for symptoms.'

I wanted to retort that I had been checked twice in the last two days, but said, 'I guess it's fine. No harm being doubly sure. It will put their mind at ease.'

'Yes. Without that, even…'

She didn't finish, but I knew what she was about to say.

I kept a distance from everyone all morning and reminded them to be especially careful about it when Seema came by.

Around ten o'clock, I wore my mask and went to sit outside on the cot. Seema arrived, looking stern, a far cry from her usual giggly self. But she couldn't maintain her expression for too long, her face breaking into a smile on seeing Gauri.

They were around the same age, Seema perhaps a little younger. The village women swore by these ASHA workers; I had seen myself how well they cared for and assisted the women of the village, during pregnancies or serious illnesses in the family – practically filling the void of doctors in remote places like ours. What they lacked in qualifications, they made up for with dedication and effort.

Seema took a thick notebook out of her bag and slipped on a pair of glasses which made her look very serious.

'*Bhaiya*, your temperature must have been checked at the station, right?'

'Yes, at both stations. They found nothing to worry about.'

She asked me questions, which I was by now familiar with, and took down notes while nodding with approval.

Finally, she put her notes back in her bag and said, 'I can see that you are fine, but the villagers are very concerned. Don't tell them I told you this, but some of them asked if it was right to allow you to come back home, till all of this had blown over. One of them even remarked that this village could suffer the fate of Haldwani, where there were no cases till someone from Delhi brought the infection with him.'

'Who said that?' I asked.

'Never mind. But people are scared and you can't blame them, can you? All day, they watch the same thing on TV, again and again. The virus may not be here yet, but they feel it is lurking outside. They are safe as long as the village is free of outsiders.'

'So I am an outsider now?'

'No, no, I didn't say that, *bhaiya*. Don't misunderstand me. But it's natural that anyone from the city will now be regarded with suspicion, no?'

Gauri said, 'I heard they refused to let Usman's brother enter the village?'

Seema nodded.

This was news to me. Usman was one of two local barbers. His brother worked somewhere in Ghaziabad.

Gauri offered Seema tea, but she refused. I saw Gauri's face darken.

'Anyway, my report will say that there is nothing to worry about. But I will return next week to check again. Sometimes, it shows up later…'

'Yes, I know. Come whenever you want, I have nothing to hide. Can I ask you something, Seema?'

'Sure.'

'God forbid, if someone did show signs of the disease, what would you do with him? Just throw him out of the village, is it?'

Seema's hand went up to her mouth.

'No! Don't say that, *bhaiya*. Provisions are being made for that too. Someone came from the DM's office in Almora to check if we have a meeting hall close by – you know, where the weddings happen? He said the nearest meeting hall would be turned into a quarantine facility with beds. I am sure there won't be a case in Basoli, but even if it does happen, arrangements will be made.'

With that, she rose and left. I sat there imagining how it would be to lie in a cot in a meeting hall, with everyone I knew a mile away. The thought filled me with dread.

Babuji emerged from his room once Seema had left.

'On the radio, they are saying our chief minister has come up with a job assistance programme.'

'Really? Like another NREGA, Babuji?' asked Gauri.

'No. From what I could make out, officials in each district will get in touch with workers returning from cities and ask them where they had previously been employed. They will then try and find these workers similar employment or offer them bank loans to start small enterprises.'

I sat up. 'For someone like me who worked in a kitchen, what would they do?'

Babuji gave this some thought, before saying, 'Maybe they can find a place for you in a hotel, like they have these Kumaon Mandal lodges, you know? But how many people can they put in there... Or they could get you a loan, so you can start a dhaba or tea shop somewhere.'

I shook my head.

'Babuji, you really think there will be tourists anytime soon? Seema was just telling us how scared they are of even *me* returning! Who is coming here on a holiday? Half these Kumaon Mandals may have to shut down for all you know, forget hiring new cooks.'

'But you and I could start a dhaba, how about that?' Gauri said with a twinkle in her eye.

I didn't have to dissuade her, Babuji did it.

'Bahu, this loan business is very tricky. When the money comes, it feels good, but it also needs to be paid back. And often, when the borrower is unable to, they take what you have and sell it.'

'Like this piece of land, the house – the only things we own,' I added.

Gauri walked back inside, looking deflated.

Morning wore into day, yet no one came to visit me. I asked Babuji about Suresh and Lalu, my Basoli friends. He said they were around, doing odd jobs when they could find any. Suresh drove someone's taxi during season sometimes, but this time there would be no season. Who knew when there would be one next? I thought of calling them but decided against it. Why put them in a spot if they didn't want to come by on their own?

When I mentioned this to Gauri, she said, 'Maybe it isn't entirely up to them. People in their families may have insisted they don't come near you. They have children, old people at home.'

I was going to tell Gauri that she sounded like she supported them, but held my tongue. I washed my clothes, watered the vegetables and then sat around doing nothing.

Babuji sensed my restlessness. 'Don't fret. It's only for a few days. After that, some work will come up. Now you are back to village life, make your peace with it,' he said.

The novelty of my arrival had also worn off for the children. Besides, they were getting tired of talking from a distance. They were too used to hanging on my arm. Children had to touch, feel, cling.

In the evening, when no one was around, I told Gauri in a low voice, 'I am actually fine, you know? Nothing is going to happen from coming close.'

'I know,' she said, before realizing what I was implying. She gave me a coy smile and covered her face with her saree.

After dinner, I whispered again to her. 'Come no, please, when they have fallen asleep?'

She shushed me and walked away.

But late that night, when I had stopped staring at the stars and closed my eyes, she came to my cot. She lay down next to me and placed a finger on my lips. It was over in seconds; I was so parched. I tried to hold her back, but she arranged her clothes and left, indicating with her hand that she would come again the next day. I smiled and fell asleep.

The days passed slowly. I noticed that Babuji was always home – he had stopped going to the village tea shop where he would sit and chat with his friends for an hour or two every day.

One day, Mohan Da called. As always, I didn't have to tell him how I was coping.

'Feels bad, right? Well, if it's any consolation, it's the same in my village. I feel like an outcast. In my father's days, there was this practice of restricting people to their huts as a method of punishment. A kind of ostracism. This feels like that.'

I asked him if there was work in his village and he echoed Babuji's words – that he would try for NREGA assignments once the two weeks were over. Then he surprised me by saying that someone from Sunauli, who worked in Delhi, had called to say that there would be demand for workers there once the lockdown was diluted. Factories were getting ready to start again, but most of the labour had left. Salaries were not bad, for people willing to join.

'You want to go again, to that well of death? Seriously, Mohan Da?'

For once, Mohan Da didn't know his mind. Of course, I didn't mention our conversation to Babuji or Gauri.

It wasn't as if nobody came to visit me. Members of the district administration came almost every day. Someone from Almora police station, an *anganwadi* worker, Seema; I didn't know that so many people from my state were even aware of my existence. I should have felt important, but felt hunted instead.

Mohan Da's words played in my head. I was trying to make my peace with village life, heeding Babuji's advice, but Mohan Da had planted the seed of a poison tree in me. I thought of Babuji's warning about the city, but also remembered that even he had gone back a second time.

It must have been on the tenth day after my return, that I was woken at night by the sound of loud coughing from Babuji's room. Nights in the village were so still, even small sounds rang out loud. At first, I thought something had caught in his throat. But no, the dry racking coughs continued. Without even thinking, my first reaction was to turn towards the other village houses. Gauri came out of the room and looked at me, alarmed. I asked her to go back inside and that we would check in the morning. Seema was expected at ten o'clock, for her third visit.

Babuji didn't emerge from his room at dawn, as he usually did. Gauri went to his door and asked how he felt. Apparently, he couldn't raise his head from the pillow. Gauri asked Sonu and Titli to remain inside their room and joined me outside.

'What shall we do? Shall we tell Seema… He has to see a doctor, right?' she asked.

'Yes, but…'

So many things were whizzing through my mind. I tried to think clearly but couldn't focus. There was this constant thudding inside my chest.

Seema came early. She always entered wearing her mask, but slipped it down to her chin once she was with us. I was about to stop her when she did it today, but couldn't.

'All well still?' she asked unsuspectingly. Any hesitation she may have felt during her first visit was gone; she was more at ease now.

I nodded and looked down. Her expression changed. She could sense something was wrong. She pulled her mask back over her nose and asked, 'The children are okay, right?'

'Yes, they are fine,' said Gauri.

And just then Babuji had another coughing fit. Long drawn out wheezes, like he was straining for breath.

Seema stood up and turned towards Gauri.

'Is that Babuji?'

'Yes.'

'Since when has he…'

'Just last night. Before that, there was nothing.'

'Does he have fever?'

'We don't know. But severe body ache, yes.'

'Oh god. And you are telling me now?'

Seema stepped away and called someone. Once the call ended, she said, 'I don't need to explain the situation to you, hopefully? An ambulance has been called for, it will be here on priority. Babuji will be taken away, all of you need to be tested properly. I mean, with throat swabs. Please keep the kids away from that room. I'll wait outside, till the ambulance arrives.'

In an hour or so, we heard the siren. It came hurtling up the village path, lights flashing. People came running out of their houses, staring at it. Then their eyes turned towards our house, where Gauri and I sat, waiting.

~

10

Essential People

'Any letters for me?' Ma asked, as Rila shuffled through the packets the guard had just brought up.

Rila answered with a straight face, 'No, Ma. Not that I can see. Why, were you expecting one?'

'I am quite sure they are misplacing Vidia's letters. I cannot imagine he hasn't written me for so long. Maybe the guards are not familiar with my name yet... Shubho, are you sure you made them write it down?'

I looked at Rila in exasperation, but she frowned back, perhaps at my impatience.

'It's sweet of him to write so regularly, no, Ma? I mean after all these years,' she said.

'Haha. Sweet isn't a word I would use for that old devil. Disparaging, that's what he was to most women, though for some reason I was spared the venom. But you are right, he has kept up over the years. Why, even after the Nobel, I was one of the first people he called. Loves burn out, friendships survive, you see.'

'That too, with all his fame. Keeping up with an old college friend this way, I think it's quite something, Ma.'

This brought a coy smile to my mother's wrinkled face. Rila was getting rather good at this game. I marvelled at my wife's patience, in indulging these absolutely insane flights of fancy.

You see, my mother is stark, raving mad. A basket case. She has been for years now. It had gotten to a point where we had to shift her to a facility in the city. Friends and people in the family judged us for it, but then they didn't have to live with her every day. And it was only getting worse. The incident with my office peon had been the last straw. She had answered the door and, when the peon asked for me, said with a straight face, 'Oh, Shubho can't meet anyone for the next fourteen days. You see, his mother passed away yesterday.'

The peon was naturally baffled, knowing she was my mother. Seeing his stunned expression, she had explained, 'You look surprised. Yes, she was in good health, but it happened suddenly. Sad.'

Her doctor had recommended the place and driven home the practicality of the arrangement. She would be less than an hour's drive away, we could meet her every week and even send meals over. And she had settled in well enough, often mistaking her fellow patients there for graduate students, lecturing them on Austen and Dickens. My mother, before it all began to unravel, was arguably the finest professor of English Literature at Bombay University, and a published poet. She was also a woman of iron will, as she needed to be, to bring the two of us – Shoma and I – up, after my father left her for some younger thing. I was 14 then, Shoma 19, my mother just about 50. She held it together for two trying decades, before the decline set in. And now, at 86, while her body had held up remarkably well, her mind had fallen prey to all the lurking shadows she had managed to hold at bay.

I told myself I had done the right thing in opting for the facility, yet there must have been some residual guilt because, on the evening the lockdown was announced, I had needed only a minute to speak to her doctor and arrange for him to call the centre, before setting off to pick her up.

We weren't going to be cut off from her for months, not knowing how safe she was there, exposed to so many patients and caregivers. If something happened, I would never forgive myself. So, she was woken up from her sleep, bundled into the car and brought home, before the shutters came down on the city. Even that night, slumped in the car with her eyes half shut, she murmured, 'I know he is here. You mean it as a surprise, but I know. He did hint at it in the last letter, but I didn't believe he would really come all the way. Then, neither of us are getting younger. I wish you had let me change into something nicer…'

Well, she had been with us for over two months now, and I would have jumped out of the window and killed myself, had it not been for Rila. Bombay apartments couldn't accommodate a mad person in full possession of her health, mobility and speech, as my dear mother was.

Thankfully, there were the stolen conversations with Martha. Once or twice, every day, I sneaked out – supposedly for smoking breaks on the street outside – and snatched a quick hello on the phone, if she could manage it. I had no idea when I would see her again. My last conversation with the HR team indicated that even if the office opened, it would be with skeletal strength for a while, which did not include support staff, especially not secretarial staff.

Reminded of her, I composed a message, carefully worded – in case it fell into the wrong hands – before turning to relieve Rila, temporarily, from my mother's clutches.

'Ma, did you do the crossword today?'

'Hah. Finished before my morning tea. Just not challenging enough, Shubho. Very soon they will get down to – three letter-word for male child. Uff! Created for dunces whose brains have been addled by smartphones.'

I rather think she had me in mind when she said this.

'Maybe I can open up more difficult puzzles for you on the laptop?'

She shook her head.

'Better to read. Speaking of which, when will Amazon start delivering books again? Whose silly idea is this distinction between essential and non-essential items – some illiterate minister, I am sure. You can order brownies and cola but not books! What good can happen to a country of such philistines?'

'What are you reading now?' I asked quickly, to divert her from this pet rant.

'The new Cromwell. Oh, Mantel. If you ever find time from your *How to Become a Better Boss* kind of tripe, maybe you can have a shot at it. Though, at the speed you read, it will probably take you a year to finish.'

Barbs, all so familiar, reserved for the dutiful son. My phone pinged, a message from Martha – free to talk? I made some excuse and stepped out of the house.

It was a hurried call – rushed endearments, almost predictable now. It ended even before I had walked down the three floors to the gate. Not feeling like a smoke, I took the lift back.

As I stepped into the flat, Ma shot me a piercing look and asked, 'Where did you go?'

'Oh, nothing, just downstairs for a minute,' I said, a bit flustered.

'Be careful, Shubho. It's your age to go about making these stupid mistakes. Just like your father.'

I was too dumbstruck to retort. At that moment, I felt I was eight again, cowering under my mother's gaze, caught out on one of my pranks. But Rila wafted in, carrying plates in her hand.

'Lunch is ready. Shubho, can you fetch some of the bowls from the kitchen?'

We sat at the table. I was dreading Ma would say something indiscreet.

But she asked, 'How is Raja holding up, Rila?'

Raja, our son, was studying at Columbia.

'Seems fine. Says he may go over to Shoma Di's for a few days. Kaushik Da may drive up to fetch him.'

Ma made a face.

'Oh, Kaushik? I still can't believe Shoma married him. Dull as ditchwater, not even good-looking.'

'Ma!' I remonstrated.

'Oh, keep quiet. How embarrassing it was to see him next to Shoma at the reception. Thank God, at least you got together with Rila. Never forget your good fortune.'

Rila could barely suppress her giggles. Ma spoke of the wedding, which took place over 25 years ago, as if it were yesterday's event.

'There's a cyclone coming to Bombay,' I said, changing the subject.

'Really? You make it sound like a circus is coming to town. So, when? Hope it isn't like the one in Calcutta.'

'No, they are saying it won't be that bad.'

Suddenly, Ma's face was transformed. Her eyes dilated, as if to instill fear in her audience, she recited:

'The wagons quickened on the streets/The thunder hurried slow/The lightning showed a yellow beak/And then a livid claw.'

It was poetry day, I imagined. I tried to guess who the lines were by but couldn't. Instead, I said, 'What a spell we are having though – epidemic, earthquakes, cyclones, locust attacks – wonder what's next.'

'Things fall apart, the centre cannot hold,' said Ma, in an ominous tone, ladling some curry on to her plate.

Her appetite never ceased to surprise me. She ate everything that was offered to her, praising what she liked, holding comment on what she didn't. If *I* ever over-salted something though, she didn't spare me her tongue.

'Some ice cream, Ma?' I asked, when the plates had been cleared.

'Why not? An essential item, after all.'

Ma liked to rest in the afternoons. We were thankful for that as it gave us some respite. So many years we had lived together under one roof – the two of us, Ma, and Raja. Then, Raja left for college, Ma went into care, and it took us no time to get used to the idea, and ease, of being on our own. It made me wonder how long the current arrangement would last... when we would feel safe to send Ma back to the facility again. When I mentioned this to Rila, she snapped at me.

'Amazing. She's *my* mother, I am the one who is broaching the subject of sending her back, and you are biting my head off!'

'Happens. Sometimes we are more caring about others than our own.'

At this, I fell silent, for her words seemed to contain a trace of accusation, perhaps unintended.

'I guess it will coincide with you rejoining office, right? Once that happens, we will know that things are somewhere close to normal.'

'Yes. And then for you to be alone with her all the time…'

'That's okay. Really. I used to think that it makes no difference to her, where she is, but seeing her here, I feel it does. I didn't tell you, but I saw her leafing through Raja's stamp albums the other day and she looked so low. I went and sat next to her and you know what she said?'

'What?'

'That Raja reminded her of you as a boy. She said you were crazy about collecting things too – matchbox covers, cold drink bottle caps with images inside – and that you would fly into a rage if Shoma Di ever touched any of that.'

'She remembers all that?'

'Oh, you will be surprised at what she remembers.'

This made me sad, as I knew all her recollections couldn't be happy; though I wasn't sure how much she would have shared with Rila. I marvelled at what a thing the mind was; how so many alternate realities could coexist in it, leaping across time and space.

'Does she ever talk about Baba?'

'Yes.'

'With spite?'

'No, not at all. The opposite, actually.'

'Oh.' I waited for her to open up. Perhaps she felt that any talk about my father would be too hurtful for me.

But, being Rila, she broke in gently. 'She says your father was jealous of you know who, though without reason.'

'What? Oh, Vidia... Come on Rila, I meant does she ever speak about real stuff?'

'She says she feels sorry for your father, for the mistakes he made. She would have forgiven him, but he didn't think she would. He never asked. Then it was too late to put things back. He must have suffered, too, she says, though the mistakes were all his.'

Rila said this and left me alone, and I was glad for it. So, Ma would have forgiven Baba. Would we have, Shoma and I? I tried to recall the time when he moved out of our home.

It happened so suddenly. I didn't remember any showdowns between my parents. There had been no previous indication that something was wrong. I wondered if Ma had any inkling either. Perhaps not.

For some time, he just vanished from our lives, leaving us to deal with the aftermath. The house felt like one where someone had died. We could see Ma was stricken with grief, though she always tried to hide it from us. Only once, when Baba called – months later – and I went to meet him somewhere, I remember how upset she became. Shoma screamed and cursed, Ma just wouldn't speak to me for days after. Something snapped between us that day, maybe she felt I took sides. Years pass, hurts are forgiven, forgotten, yet sometimes they remain, lodged inside us like shrapnel.

When Ma emerged from her room, dishevelled from sleep, she looked more like the patient at the care home. Vulnerable, no longer the smart old lady with her acerbic wit and smart comebacks. Rila guided her to the sofa and sat behind her, gently combing her sparse hair. Ma's eyes closed with comfort. Then Rila placed a hand on Ma's shoulder, and rose and fetched tea from the kitchen, along with two

Shrewsbury biscuits on a plate. I looked on, as if under a spell, unable to fathom the heaviness that gathered in me.

In the evening, I asked Ma if she wanted a small glass of something. Sometimes, she would join us for a drink. She accepted a small Campari with soda, asked me to play 'Ruby Tuesday' on the stereo, and we sat in the drawing room, sipping our drinks.

'When is your cyclone due?' she asked.

'Wednesday, they are saying. But maybe it won't turn up, or won't hit the city, who knows?'

'Yes, nature is like us, full of surprises. Listen, before it strikes, can you take me back to my place once?'

It stung, to hear her describe the care facility as her place, but I let it pass.

'Why there?' I asked without showing my surprise.

'I need to get the girls started on Woolf. Slackers, each of them. They must have stopped reading altogether with me gone. Besides…'

'What?'

'My letters from Vidia are all lying there. I wouldn't want them falling into someone's hands, would I? No one cares about me, but he has a reputation, right? And that Sarla, she knows there is something precious inside that cabinet of mine. Twice she has asked me about it. Always sniffing about for some gossip.'

'I'll ask the warden to lock your room.'

'Who? Old Kamble? From the frying pan to the fire, huh. Do you know his past? The man spent 10 years in prison! For poisoning his wife. And now he is supposed to be in charge of our safe-keeping. Miracle we are still alive…'

'Let all this be, Ma. Tell us something about your childhood,' Rila said.

It was her habit to prod Ma about old recollections every time she had a drink with us.

Ma laughed. 'My childhood? Do you mean the freedom struggle then?'

I could see that the drink had revived her, the sarcasm was back.

'Ma! Something about your youth, college days, your writing, maybe.'

I braced for another biting comment, but a strange smile alighted on her face.

'Shubho, go to the room and get my bag. The green one, not the money purse.'

When I fetched it, she opened one of the flaps and produced a photograph.

'Here, the story of my youth. They say a picture is worth a thousand words,' she said, handing it to Rila.

I walked across and stood behind Rila. She held a black and white photo, discoloured with age, of a striking looking woman. It was Ma standing between two men on what looked like the grounds of an Oxford campus. Rila pointed at one of the men and looked up at me; I nodded. It was Baba. She had seen him only once, when I took her across to meet him, just before our marriage. I was surprised she recognized him, as in the picture, he was a lean boy with sunken cheeks and a full crown of hair. The man she had met was bald, with a salt and pepper goatee.

'Ma, how absolutely stunning you look!' Rila gushed. 'How come I have never seen this picture before?'

'It was lying in this house, inside one of my old books. I just found it the other day. Was surprised myself, didn't know it still existed.'

'Who's the... other man with you?'

Ma smiled in a way that made her look like a naughty child.

'The *other* man, as you call him, is Billy. William Cartwright. Took PPE at our college; Shubho's father and he were inseparable.

Billy thought Rudra was a genius, and I the most exotic creature he ever laid eyes on. Indophile, you see, born in Madras.'

'How interesting. Strange you never mentioned him before,' I said.

Ma gave me a look.

'Because you had no interest in my past, dear. Shoma knows.'

I must have looked at her in an odd way at that last bit, because she snapped, 'Now don't start getting ideas in your head. This was no ménage à trois. We were all friends.'

'Come on, Ma,' Rila said, in a teasing voice, which I would never dare try on her.

'What do I say, Rila, it all seems like another lifetime now. But there was this one time we went to a party – Rudra and I were seeing each other by then – where Billy got drunk and asked me to dance with him. It was a harmless twirl, but I remember how crushed Shubho's father looked, as if I had betrayed him. That day, I decided I would be a one-man woman. Fat lot of good it did me in the end.'

She laughed and took the picture back from Rila.

'I can't see myself in Shoma, you know. Only the forehead...'

She was getting tired, I could see. I gestured to Rila and she walked to the kitchen to fetch Ma's glass of milk. Ma stood up.

'Goodnight then. It felt nice to talk about Billy after so long. And Rila, he would have fallen for you in a flash,' she said, brushing Rila's arm with her fingers in a rare show of affection.

After dinner, Rila and I sat staring at the photograph. She was right, I had forgotten how beautiful Ma had been, in her day. Strange how my memory of her was dominated by the difficult years – the way her personality changed, practically overnight, from the shock of that reckless betrayal. The task of running the family – she was too proud to ever accept any help from Baba – and providing for us, our education, may have armed her with a much-needed sense of purpose, leaving little time to sit around and mope, but it also hardened her. She became a machine, not the woman we knew before, more so once Shoma left for university. How unfortunate, I thought, looking at the young girl in the photograph, that in my mind's eye she was never the woman from the time we were a happy unit. She would be gone soon and I felt I owed it to her to remember her in a better light.

'It's sweet how fondly she still speaks of your father, despite…' Rila said.

'Yes, though I wonder if it's because she remembers only the time when things were good between them, not the later years. You know they say that about her condition.'

'I don't think so. She has probably let it all go, the bitterness. It happens at an age, when you are nearer to the end.'

The words hung between us. I tried to lighten things up with a flippant comment.

'I wish she spared some of that sweetness for me, not bite my head off all the time.'

'Oh, come on. That's her way of showing affection. You don't get it, do you? It may seem she is fonder of me, but if I ever did the wrong thing by you, she would gouge my eyes out, make no mistake!'

'And would you?'

'What?'

'Do the wrong thing by me…'

Rila looked into my eyes and said, 'I may not possess your mother's beauty, but her loyalty, certainly.'

A flush crept up my neck. I had to lower my eyes for a moment.

The next morning, I called Martha and told her it was off between us. It wasn't easy, but I gave it to her straight, and didn't beat around the bush. There were no tantrums. She accepted my apology and said she understood. Maybe she was relieved. After all, illicit passion is a fire that needs to be fed.

When I returned, Ma and Rila were in the room, drinking tea.

Ma looked up and said, 'You know, Shubho, I was just telling Rila that if Vidia were to suddenly pass away, no one would even inform me at the centre. I cannot bear the thought of hearing about it later, from someone.'

She shook her head, looking truly distraught.